A very specific image is brought to mind when we hear the word Christmas. This image usually includes family and friends gathering around a tree. One particular tradition has been largely forgotten. Very few people today see ghost stories as part of that picture. Christmas is supposed to be a festive time of year, how do ghost stories fit into the picture?

The popular notion is that tales of supernatural terrors don't belong to the Ideal of Christmas. The truth is ghost stories were a Christmas tradition dating back as far as the nineteenth century. In fact one of the most beloved Christmas stories of all time is about a man who is being tormented by supernatural forces. Another example comes from the English writer M. R. James who published several volumes of ghost stories that he originally told as Christmas Eve entertainment for parties. Few if any of James's ghost stories were set during Christmas, but for a long time his tales were strongly tied to the holiday itself. There are dozens of other examples including the famous poem "The Raven", written by Edgar Allan Poe. Many people decide to recite the poem during

October, but as it is written the events take place "In the bleak December".

I could go on with examples of the tradition, but there is little point since it has been marginalized in today's world of candy canes and Santa Clause. Charles Dickens' classic has been adapted for stage and screen countless times, but there are very few who even realize that they are indeed watching a ghost story. (This is sad considering that there are characters that actually have Ghost as part of their names.) Needless to say the ghost story has all but lost its place in the Christmas season. Some think it is probably for the best but I for one disagree.

I got the Idea for this collection one December evening a few years ago. I had just listened to a rendition of one of James' stories and the reader explained the background of many of James' works. The idea of writing Christmas themed ghost stories fascinated me. I did a little research and decided that I should give it a try. I even decided to name the stories after some of my favorite Christmas songs. From that point it was just a matter of deciding what kind of stories I wanted to do.

Christmas Spirits Rueckert

One thing that I knew for certain was that I didn't want to write any stories about Santa Clause, Frosty the Snowman, or any of the other pop culture parts of the holiday. At first I had planned to tie each story of the collection to one another, but I eventually decided that it would be wiser to just write a collection of stories. As a result you will see threads that tie stories together in a few arcs. There are also a few stand alone stories that I think enrich the collection as a whole.

In the pages of this collection you will find ghosts of all shapes and sizes; from the mysterious Man in Black who seems to be around every corner, to the old man that just wants to spend Christmas with his family. Weather you prefer helpful spirits or terrible specters this is the book for you. So sit back in your chair, sip some hot chocolate and try to get into the Christmas Spirit.

Baby its Cold Outside

Larry Saunders looked at the battered television screen and swallowed a lump in his throat. There was no doubt in his mind that the person on the screen was his wife Janet. He expected to see her smile and sit up on the gurney and tell him it was just a practical joke. She had told him she would get him back for pretending to cut his thumb off while carving the thanksgiving turkey. But the longer he looked at her still face he knew for a fact that his wife was dead. He looked at the morgue attendant and nodded.

"Do you need a moment Mr. Saunders? I can step out in the hall to give you some time."

Larry tried to speak but his throat double clutched and the lump in his throat forced its way back up. He nearly broke out in tears and sat down heavily on the only chair in the room. The attendant started to walk towards the door but Larry grabbed him by his wrist to stop him. After what felt like an eternity he got himself under control and asked the only question he could think of. "What happened?"

"We don't have many of the details but the police officer that called in the coroner told us that they found her in her car. So far the guess is that she went off the road in the storm a few nights ago, her car is totaled and they had to cut her out. They said she was on one of the side streets and no one plowed it till this morning. That's when they found her."

"Did she suffer?"

"Her body was frozen but the Coroner says that she most likely suffered a broken neck in the crash, Death would have been instantaneous. It's not much consolation but it seems like she died without feeling any pain. I am sorry for your loss Mr. Saunders." The attendant put a hand on Larry's shoulder. The gesture felt robotic, as though he had done it a million times before. Larry looked at his wife's face on the screen again and the lump in his throat threatened to strangle him before he was able to swallow it back down.

To Larry the next hour and a half was a haze. The only thing in his mind was the image of his wife's face on that screen. He vaguely remembered being asked to sign some papers and there was a brief discussion about which funeral home the body should be delivered to. The morgue attendant referring to his wife as "the body" hit Larry like a ton of bricks. He confessed to the attendant that he didn't remember Janet telling him what she wanted to do when one of them died. They had only been married for two years and thought they would have more time to figure it out. The decision was put off until Larry could talk to his in-laws about the arrangements. After the paperwork was signed he took one last look at his wife's body before leaving the morgue.

On his way out the door the attendant handed Larry his wife's luggage to take home with him. The large wheeled suitcase was so battered that Larry hardly recognized it. Janet had been on her way to a business meeting in Michigan three days before. He knew something was wrong when she didn't call him that night to check in, but the police told him that he had to wait twenty-four hours before he could declare her missing. Deep down he had hoped that they would find her snowed in at some hotel along the highway. Larry pushed the memories away and tossed the battered suitcase into his trunk.

When Larry got into his car he looked at his telephone. There was a missed call from his father-in-law. Janet's parents had been calling at least twice a day since the day she went missing. They kept telling him to keep up hope that she would turn up eventually. Janet's mother said she probably forgot to pack her phone charger and let the battery die. It is true that she was sometimes forgetful but deep down Larry knew something wasn't right. He looked at the screen of his phone and tried to find the words to tell his in-laws what had happened. In that moment Larry went through so many conflicting emotions that his head felt like it was about to explode. Finally he took a deep breath and thumbed the "Send" Key on his phone. His father-in-law answered after the third ring and Larry told him "They found her, it's not good."

The sun had set when Larry got home. The conversation with his in-laws was one of the hardest things he had to do in his entire life. How do you tell someone that their daughter died in her car all alone? Larry barely held it together when Janet's mother started crying. After his Mother-in-law calmed down they decided to meet in the morning and discuss the arrangements. Larry didn't know what to do after he hung up the phone. He didn't want to go home so He drove around town for an hour trying to work up the courage. Eventually he stopped at Janet's favorite restaurant. He tried to eat dinner but nothing seemed appetizing. Eventually he gave up and went home.

The house was full of memories of his life with Janet. Every single room held traces of her. She loved decorating the house, especially when it was time to put up the Christmas decorations. He looked at the lights strung around the garage door and shook his head. He remembered telling her to be careful when she climbed the rickety old ladder in the garage when she was putting them up. She just smiled and told him to hold the latter and stop staring at her ass. The memory made Larry smile for a moment, but it was cut short when his mind went back to his wife's face on the beat up monitor.

Christmas Spirits Rueckert

Larry walked into the dark house alone and went straight to the living room without turning on any lights. The sound of his footsteps echoing on the hardwood floor opened the floodgates that had been holding by a thread since the moment he first got the call from the morgue. Larry's knees buckled under the weight of his grief and he fell to the floor sobbing. He curled into himself and let loose all the emotions that had been building inside of him with a pained scream. All of the worries and the three nights of not knowing where she was, compiled with the shock and horror of seeing his wife's dead face on a screen poured out of Larry in a flood of tears. He cried for what felt like an eternity before he was able to get control of himself. Finally he was able to get to his hands and knees and crawl to the couch where he fell into a deep sleep.

That night he dreamed that he was back in the morgue, but this time rather than looking at Janet through a television screen he was in the room sitting next to her body. Her skin was tinted blue from the cold and there were patches of frost in the corners of her eyes. After a moment Larry could swear he saw his wife's chest rise and fall beneath the sheet that was covering her body. He stood up and walked closer to the gurney to look.

"Janet?" He asked softly, simultaneously hoping that she would and would not answer. But to his surprise they eyes of his dead wife opened. Larry stumbled backward and fell to the floor as Janet sat up on the gurney and held the sheet across her chest. Even in death his wife showed signs of modesty. Janet looked down at Larry with a mixture of sadness and pity.

"Hi Larry," She said with a faint smile as she looked down at him.

"Janet…"

"I'm cold Larry, will you hold me?" Janet opened her arms to him. Larry stood up and hugged her as tight as he could. Her skin was frozen solid but he didn't care, she was in his arms and he never wanted to let go. As the two embraced Janet's frozen skin began to grow warmer. After a while she began to move in her husband's arms. He released her for a moment and looked in her face. "I'm still so cold Larry, please don't let them put me outside

It's so cold out there. You know how much I hate the cold." She shivered visibly, a tear slid down her cheek and froze in place. Larry wiped his hand across the tear and brushed it away as best as possible before wrapping his arms around Janet again.

When Larry woke up he was lying on the couch wrapped in a blanket. He looked at the clock over the fireplace and saw that it was three thirty in the morning. The thought of climbing into the bed he shared with Janet made Larry shudder. Instead he set the alarm on his phone and went back to sleep on the couch and by morning he forgot all about the strange dream.

The meeting with the funeral director and Janet's parents was awkward. Larry tried to be helpful but his Father-in-law ended up making most of the arrangements. Even though Larry wanted to hear all of the options his in-laws seemed to have their minds made up what was to be done with her remains. Ultimately the decision was made that Janet would be buried in her family plot at the cemetery. After that it was just a matter of picking a coffin and setting up music and times. The funeral would be held on the twenty third of December so that no one would miss out on

Christmas. Larry found little solace in the decision but understood the desire not to ruin everyone's holiday.

Throughout the entire meeting something wasn't sitting right with Larry. At first he thought it was just the thought of Janet actually being dead. It wasn't until the funeral director mentioned the fact that since the ground was frozen and the body would have to be kept in cold storage until burial that it struck him.

"Is there any other option? Janet hates being cold." Larry said to the funeral director.

"I understand the desire to hold on to your spouse by putting attributes of your life together onto the deceased. But your wife is dead, what is left is just a shell of the woman you loved. I don't think the cold will bother her all that much now Mr. Saunders. We already discussed cremation and you seemed to agree to the burial option."

Larry wanted to say something but one look at his Mother-in-law shut his mouth. The fact remained that Janet was dead. It wouldn't matter if her remains were in a freezer for a while. If burial gave his wife's parents a little bit of closure it was probably for the best. The calling hours would be in two days and the funeral the following morning. Then Janet's body would go into cold storage.

"Just make sure she is somewhere nice."

The rest of the day was spent planning the funeral and fielding phone calls from friends and family. The decision was made to play some of Janet's favorite Christmas songs since she died so close to the holiday. The rest of the plans fell into place just as smoothly. Janet's mother wanted to pick out the outfit that she would be buried in but Larry wouldn't allow it. He didn't want to see his wife in one of her business suits looking stern and matronly. He wanted to see her how she really was, beautiful and full of energy. When his in-laws left Larry went into the closet and pulled out Janet's favorite dress. He held the fabric close to his face and breathed in her scent before laying the dress on the bed. The smell brought a fresh wave of tears to his eyes. The hardest part of the outfit was picking the right accessories. Larry remembered Janet matching everything effortlessly, but he found it difficult to know what matched with what outfit. Eventually he pieced together something that he thought his wife would wear. The crowning touch was the Silver pendant he had given her on their first Christmas together.

When everything was set Larry looked out the window and saw that the sun had set and a fresh blanket of snow covered the ground. Suddenly Larry felt very tired and was about to fall asleep when he thought he heard music. The sound was coming from the stereo system in the living room downstairs. He walked down to the room but found no one else in the house but himself. The radio was playing one of Janet's Christmas CD's that they used to pick music for the funeral. It took Larry a second to recognize the voices of Diana Shore and Buddy Clark singing "Baby its cold outside".

The song recalled Larry to his dream of the night before. He shuddered when he remembered Janet telling him not to let them put her out in the cold. The image of her beautiful face with frost in the corners of her eyes and mouth He quickly walked over to the stereo and pressed the power button. The unit shut down instantly and Larry turned around to go back upstairs but froze when he saw his reflection in the nearby window. Janet was standing behind him in the room. But she didn't look like the woman that he had married. Her skin was a frosty blue, and her long hair dangled with Icicles. She wore a horrible expression that chilled Larry's blood in his veins. The unblinking eyes stared at him with an expression of outrage and fear.

Larry spun around to face the apparition but the room behind him was empty. He took a few deep breaths and started to rationalize what he thought he saw. The song reminded him of his dream which made him hallucinate. Or maybe he saw a snow covered tree in the back yard and his eyes played a trick on him. There was no way his dead wife could have been in the room, her body was locked in the funeral parlor across town. Eventually Larry had convinced himself that he had imagined the whole thing. He even convinced himself that he had forgotten to turn off the stereo system when he went upstairs to get Janet's dress. He was so absorbed in putting together the outfit he just didn't hear the other songs on the record playing. It was just coincidence that the

song had been playing when he became aware of the music.

When he finally went back upstairs Larry undressed and

climbed into the queen sized bed he had once shared with his wife.

He pulled the blankets up over his head and tried to fall asleep. He

tossed and turned trying to find a comfortable position, but nothing

seemed to help. After an hour of trying to sleep Larry decided that

the bed was just too big for one person. It just felt wrong to sleep

in it without his wife. He grabbed a pillow and blanket and went

back down to the couch in the living room where he had slept the

night before. It didn't take long to get himself situated on the

couch and fall asleep.

Larry woke up to the sound of Janet whispering his name.

He sat up on the couch and looked around. After a moment he

remembered where he was and lied back down. He must have been

dreaming he told himself, but before he went back to sleep he

heard her again. The sound was coming from the back porch. Larry

got up and walked to the sliding glass door and peered through the blinds. The night was silent and still. There was no trace of life outside the house.

For a moment Larry thought about opening the door and looking outside but changed his mind when he saw frost on the inside handle. The cold night air had most likely frozen the door shut so even trying to open it would be a useless effort. Larry went back to the couch and wrapped himself tightly in the blanket to ward off the cold night air. He looked at the clock on the mantle and saw that it read three thirty in the morning just like it had the previous night. He shrugged it off as coincidence and curled up and went back to sleep.

The next morning Larry was awakened by the doorbell ringing. He looked at the clock on the mantle; it was nine o clock in the morning. Larry wondered who would be visiting at this hour. His muscles groaned in protest as he rose to his feet and shuffled to the front door. When he opened it he was face to face with the elderly neighbor Mrs. Mclusky. The older woman was holding a casserole tray in front of her.

"I'm sorry to call so early, but I heard about your loss yesterday and Thought I would bring you a little something to eat." Mrs. Mclusky smiled and offered Larry the casserole dish which he took with a weak smile.

"Thank you Mrs. M. I appreciate the thought but you didn't have to."

"Hush you," the older woman said with a wave of her hand. "I remember when My Albert died God rest him. I couldn't cook for a week. Your wife made me dinner every day that week. And I know how you men are when there is no one around to look after you. Janet would want to know that you are being taken care of."

"Okay Mrs. M." Larry replied, "Would you like to come inside? I was just about to start a pot of tea." Mrs. Mclusky accepted the invitation and the pair spent the morning sitting at the table and talking about Janet.

"How are you holding up Mr. Saunders?" The older woman asked as though she had been putting off asking until the proper moment.

"As well as can be expected I guess, you know Janet had been missing for a few days before they found her body. I think deep down I knew that first night that she was gone. That doesn't make it any easier to accept that she's gone." Larry's eyes began to fill with tears and the old woman patted his hands reassuringly.

"It's that way with two people so in love. I remember when Albert drew his last breath it was like a part of me died along with him. I never did get that part of me back but don't you worry Mr. Saunders, it might not seem like it now but that hurt does get easier to deal with."

The teapot began to whistle and Mrs. Mclusky stood up and walked over to the stove. Larry began to rise but the older woman waved him back to his seat. "You just sit there and relax Mr. Saunders. Let me take care of the tea." Larry sat back down and watched her poor the tea. While she worked the older woman began to hum a familiar tune. It took Larry a second to place it but when he did a chill ran up his spine. She was humming the same song that had started playing the night before. The one that made Larry think he saw his dead frozen wife in his reflection.

When Mrs. Mclusky turned around she gasped to see Larry's face turn so pale. She automatically stopped humming and ran over to check his forehead. "Are you feeling alright Mr. Saunders? You look a little pale." She asked in a worried voice that made Larry feel ashamed of his reaction.

"Yeah Mrs. M I'm Fine," He replied sheepishly. "It's just that song; it makes me think of how Janet died."

"Oh dear I'm so sorry Mr. Saunders." The older woman said coloring a bit. She was clearly embarrassed at causing him any kind of distress. "I didn't even think of it. What a horrible song especially with the circumstances and all. I should go." Mrs. Mclusky put down the tea cups and wiped her hands off on a towel.

"No, it's ok Mrs. M, I'm Fine. Please sit down and we'll have our tea." Larry stood up and tried to calm the older woman as she started for the door.

"No, I really should be going. I have other things I need to do today any way. I will bring you some dinner tomorrow if that's alright." Mrs. Mclusky made her way to the front door and opened it. Larry followed her and stopped in his tracks. Janet was standing just outside the door shivering in the cold morning air. Her eyes pleaded with Larry, but he couldn't think of anything that he could do to help her.

Mrs. Mclusky didn't seem to notice anything out of the ordinary. The older woman just pulled her coat on and walked out onto the porch and through the spectral woman. When Mrs. Mclusky passed through Janet the specter evaporated like a puff of exhaled breath.

It was starting to snow when Larry got in his car to drive to the funeral parlor to drop off the things he had picked out. By the time he parked his car in the lot the gentle flurry had given way to a heavy dusting of white.

When Larry dropped off the clothes and jewelry the receptionist told him that the funeral director had asked to speak to him if that was alright. She escorted him to the office and knocked on the door before opening it. The funeral director rose from his desk and offered Larry his hand.

"Thank you for seeing me again Mr. Saunders." He said with the same polite smile that he had given the day before. Larry took his hand and nodded.

"What was it that you wanted to see me about?"

"It seemed to me that you were less than happy with the arrangements made for your wife's funeral. I just wanted to let you know that since you are listed as the primary beneficiary in Janet's will you can change any of the plans if you feel that you need to." The director looked at Larry over his glasses questioningly. "Are there any arrangements that you would like to change Mr. Saunders?"

"No, everything is fine just how it is. It means a lot to Janet's parents to have her in the family plot so I guess it's for the best."

The funeral director nodded and handed him a card. "Well, just in case you change your mind you can give me a call any time." Larry took the card and left the funeral parlor.

The drive home took twice as long as the drive to the funeral parlor. The snow had increase, which made driving difficult. Larry slipped on patches of black ice twice as he drove. When Larry finally got home his nerves were so worked up that he was exhausted. He walked into the house and sat down hard on his easy chair and must have dozed off.

Suddenly Larry thought he heard someone say his name very softly. He opened his eyes and looked around the room. When he saw that he was the only person in the room he laid his head back down and closed his eyes again. He heard his name again, this time the voice was louder and more forceful. Larry got out of his chair and walked into the next room. The voice came again, this time Larry recognized it as Janet's voice.

"Janet?" Larry said to the empty room. "Janet, are you here?" He was answered by a cold breeze that made goose bumps rise on his arms and legs as it circled his body.

"Larry I'm co cold." Janet's voice seemed to come from all around the room. Larry's heart broke to hear his wife sound so unhappy.

"How can I help you?"

"Don't let them put me outside Baby; it's so cold out there. I don't want to be cold anymore." The temperature in the room dropped further. When Larry exhaled he could see his own breath. He wrapped his arms around himself but the cold bit deep into him. "I've been so cold Larry. I'm still so cold, please help me."

"They want to bury you in the family plot."

"No!" The reply was so forceful that it resonated through the room and made Larry covers his ears. The temperature dropped yet again and Larry thought he wouldn't be able to bear it anymore, but just as suddenly the room grew warm again. Larry was not surprised when he heard the music start again in the other room. He walked over to the stereo, but before he turned off the song, he picked up the phone and called the funeral home.

An hour after his conversation with the funeral director, Janet's Father called. Larry prepared himself for an angry tirade when he answered the phone. Instead when he put the receiver to his ear he was greeted by a calm and collected voice on the other end.

"Is there something you want to tell me Larry?" his father-in-law asked quietly.

"I'm guessing you heard that I changed the burial plans today." He could hardly contain his confusion at the simple and direct question.

"I just got off the phone with the funeral director. He told me you decided to have Janet's body cremated." Larry listened for any traces of anger in the voice of his father-in-law but couldn't find any.

"Yes I know you guys wanted to put her in your family plot but I thought that she would have wanted it this way." Larry switched the phone from one year to the other. "I'm sorry if that upset you but it just didn't seem right to put her in the ground."

"I understand." His father-in-law answered. "Janet was your wife Larry. If you think this is best then this is what we will do. We'll still have the calling hours tomorrow." Something in his voice made Larry suspicious. Both men knew something that neither of them was talking about. Eventually he had to ask the obvious question.

"Are you alright? I was expecting you to be more upset about me changing the plans."

"I was at first but the more I thought about it I realized you did the right thing. Janet always hated being cold, even when she was a little girl she would sleep with a heavy blanket almost year round. I don't know that she would ever rest in peace in the cold ground." At that moment Larry realized exactly why Janet's father wasn't upset with him.

"I haven't been sleeping well; I keep dreaming that Janet is talking to me. Have you had any strange dreams lately?"

The line was quiet for a moment before Janet's father answered. It was obvious that he was choosing his words carefully. "I don't know if you would call them dreams or just feelings Larry. But I admit I haven't been sleeping too well myself." The two talked for a while longer before Larry made an excuse to end the conversation. Before the conversation ended Janet's father- in- law got quiet for a second before he spoke again.

"I don't think people would believe us if we told them about these dreams Larry. It's probably best that we not talk about them. Janet's soul should be allowed to rest in peace." Larry was about to reply when the phone disconnected. He decided that his father -in- law was probably right. Janet should be allowed to rest in peace and that wouldn't happen if he dwelt on the strange events of the last few days. That night Larry slept without waking up once.

The calling hours and funeral were tasteful and appropriate. It seemed like everyone had a pleasant story to share about Janet. Larry looked at his wife and marveled at how different she looked from the woman he had seen on that battered television screen only a few short days before. She looked like the woman he fell in love with all those years ago. The sight made his heart ache but Larry knew that Janet was in a better place. The director asked Larry if he wanted to be present for the cremation but he didn't think he could handle that.

After the funeral Larry went to stay the night with Janet's parents. It felt good not to be alone in the house that felt too big. He spent the night looking at Janet's high school pictures. It was strangely comfortable to be this close to her after the funeral. When Christmas Eve came, the three sat around the living room staring at the decorated tree.

"When did they say you would get the ashes?" Janet's Mother asked after a short silence.

"The funeral director said they would be delivered in about a week."

"What are you going to do when you get them?" Larry sat for a moment contemplating his hot chocolate before he answered.

Christmas Spirits Rueckert

"I think I'm going to keep her over the fire place for a while. Then I'll take her somewhere where it never gets cold and scatter her ashes. I think that she would like that."

That June Larry took a vacation in Hawaii where he and Janet went on their honeymoon. He spent most of the week on the beach watching the wave's crash and thinking about Janet. On the last day before he left he took the urn he had been given up to the top of one of the volcanoes on the Island of Honolulu. He opened the urn and slowly emptied its contents. The wind took Janet's ashes and scattered them across the volcano. Larry closed his eyes and let the warm breeze blow through his hair. Off in the distance he thought he heard Janet whisper his name. He stood for a few more minutes watching his wife's ashes swirl in the wind before he turned around and walked down the mountain towards the sea.

Auld Lang Zine

Patrick stood in front of the worn down commercial building and shook his head with disbelief. This didn't look like the place to find the wildest Christmas party of the year. It looked more like the setting for a war movie. Most of the building's glass had been shattered ages ago, leaving only jagged shards in their place. There was so much graffiti on the walls that Patrick wasn't sure what color the building had originally been. Even the front door had seen better days; it swung on its one remaining hinge with every puff of wind that blew past it. Right next to where Patrick was standing there was a post that had at one time held a business sign but the sign had been taken down years ago.

Somewhere in the back of his mind Patrick thought he could hear a voice telling him that this was a bad idea. He carefully re-read the address from the flier to make sure that they matched up. There was no mistake; he had found the right place. Now he just had to convince himself to go inside.

Patrick had moved from Michigan just weeks before the holidays. Since then he had dedicated almost all of his time to getting ahead at his new job. It had been hard to meet new people since he moved to town. Aside from the one's he had met at work that is. So when someone had left a flier for "The Christmas party of the century" on his windshield he decided he might as well check it out. "Who knows," he told himself. "Maybe this will turn out to be the first step to a whole new life. It's not like I'm doing anything else for the holidays."

The thought reminded Patrick of the life he had left behind when he moved. His family tried to convince him not to leave. Everyone wanted him to stay and help manage the family store. They tried to tell him that he wouldn't make it in the city on his own, but Patrick couldn't stand another minute of his small town

life. He studied hard and got a job offer during his last semester.
On the day he graduated from college Patrick packed up his old
VW van and left his old life behind.

As Patrick stood there trying to decide whether or not to go
inside he noticed movement out of the corner of his eye. He turned
his head slightly and noticed an attractive young woman in a red
dress and heels walking towards him. She was holding a flier
identical to the one in his hand. She stopped in front of him and
smiled.

"Are you here for the party too?" She asked in a whisper.
Her eyes darted to the front door of a dilapidated building. There
was something about her that drew Patrick's attention, but he
couldn't pinpoint just what it was.

"I guess so." Patrick answered after a few seconds. He was
trying to alleviate his own doubts as much as those of the young
woman. Her smile widened and she started towards the door. After
a few steps she looked over her shoulder at Patrick.

"Come on lazy bones," She shouted back at him excitedly. "You don't want to miss all of the fun do you?" Then with a wicked smile she threw open the door and ran inside. Patrick stood dumbfounded for a moment before he finally walked up the rickety steps to the door. The voice in his head grew louder, but he ignored it. If the girl in the red dress wasn't afraid to go in, then nether was he.

When he got inside Patrick was shocked to see that the interior of the building looked nothing like he had expected. Instead of reflecting the ruins of the exterior everything inside was clean and brightly lit. Brightly colored decorations covered the walls and ceiling of a large foyer, there a tree in one corner of the room decorated with silver ornaments. On top of the tree was a five pointed star with precious stones at each of the corners. On one end of the room was a long table stacked high with refreshments. Christmas music played throughout the building, and dozens of people whirled around on the dance floor.

There was only one thing in the room that didn't fit with the festive decor. In the back of the room stood a tall grandfather clock made of dark ebony. The dancers ignored the click of pendulum as it kept time with the music. A chill ran up Patrick's spine and he had to force himself to look away from the clock.

Patrick looked around the brightly lit room for the girl in the red dress. He knew that she had to be in here somewhere. For several minutes he scanned the crowded dance floor in search of her. Every now and then he was sure that he caught a glimpse of her red dress, but every time he thought he was catching up to her she disappeared into the crowd before he could introduce himself.

Eventually Patrick gave up his search in favor of the refreshment table. As he made his way to the long table he smiled and nodded at everyone who caught his eye. A strange apprehension arose when he noticed the way that some of the others were watching him. He felt their eyes burn into him like lasers. Patrick told himself that it was all in his imagination and pushed the thought aside with a laugh. The voice he thought he had heard earlier was telling him that he should leave, but again Patrick pushed the thought aside. If these people didn't want him here then they wouldn't have posted fliers all over town advertising this party.

By the time he had gotten to the table the only thing on Patrick's mind was food. He had even forgotten about the girl in the red dress. The table was covered in gingerbread cookies and candy canes among other amazing looking snacks. Patrick helped himself to a little bit of everything and then made his way to the punchbowl. He filled a glass with the red liquid and took a sip. Almost immediately he felt warm sensation spread throughout his body. The feeling of apprehension tried to push its way back to the surface, but Patrick smothered it without a second thought. He leaned on the pillar closest to the refreshment table and watched the people dance to the music. The movements of the dancers hypnotized Patrick and he found himself humming along to the music.

"Excuse me," a familiar voice broke in through the haze and brought him back to the world around him. Patrick looked and saw the girl in the red dress smiling beside him. She was even more attractive up close and in a well lit room. Her blue eyes sparkled in the light like stars in the sky. "Excuse me," She said again.

"Yes?" Patrick replied with a smile of his own.

"Did you know that you are standing under the mistletoe?" The girl in the red dress asked. Patrick looked up and saw a small bundle of green leaves tied with a red ribbon hanging from the pillar above his head. A smile spread across his face as he looked at the girl in red again.

"Well," he replied coolly. "I guess I am. Does this mean I get a kiss from a pretty lady?"

The woman in red leaned close to Patrick and kissed him gently on the cheek. The feeling of her warm lips lingered for a few moments without fading. Then she took Patrick by the hand and led him out to the dance floor. When they got there the music had changed to a slow tempo. The girl in red put on of her hands on Patrick's shoulder and he took her by the waist. As he drew her near his head swam with the scent of her perfume. Time felt as though it were slowing down as Patrick danced with his arms wrapped around this lovely stranger. He found himself wishing that this moment would never end.

Suddenly the great clock began to chime. After ten chimes Patrick became aware of the feeling of dozens of people staring at him. He looked around the room to find that everyone had stopped what they were doing and all eyes were on Patrick and his dance partner. A small voice in the back of his mind was starting to tell him that he should leave, but the girl in red stroked the side of his face gently with her hand.

"Don't worry about them, they're all just jealous." She said in a soft voice that sounded like music in Patrick's ears. Her touch washed away all of the apprehension that had been building inside of him.

"Yeah," he replied with a smile. "I would be jealous of me too. Especially at this moment." The girl in red laughed at his words. The sound made Patrick feel weak in the knees. Gradually the other dancers resumed their partners and the room was teaming with laughter once more.

When the song switched to something with a faster tempo Patrick started to look around the room for a quiet spot that he could take his partner for a talk. When he saw an empty table over by the tree he guided the girl in red towards it. The other guests at the party made way for the pair as they moved to take a seat at the table.

"Tell me," Patrick said when the woman in red sat down opposite him. "What brings you here tonight?"

"I wanted to make a connection." She replied without taking her eyes off of him. "How about you?"

"I'm new in town and don't know many people. I thought that this would be an opportunity to fix that." His face flushed slightly as he spoke. "I don't know about you but I think I found what I came for." Patrick reached out and touched the girl in red's hand. The contact spread a warm feeling up his arm, but she pulled away before he could wrap his fingers around her hand.

"Not just yet mister." She said playfully. "I don't even know your name."

"I'm Patrick." He said as he held out his hand for her to shake. She eyed it momentarily before taking it.

"My name is Charlotte."

"Are you from around here Charlotte?" Patrick asked with a grin.

"I used to be, but I only come back to visit now. In fact I have to leave town again tonight unless something comes up." She looked at Patrick expectantly as she spoke. His heart sank when she mentioned leaving.

"I sure hope something comes up then." He said after a moment's silence.

"Me too." The tone of her voice made Patrick's heart skip a beat. The pair spoke for a while longer. Patrick told Charlotte about his family in Michigan, his job, and why he had moved so far from home. When he finished she told him a little about growing up in the city. Patrick noticed that her eyes took on a nostalgic gleam when she spoke. Even after she stopped he saw a look of sadness in her face.

"If you miss the city so much why did you ever move away?"

"I didn't have a choice," She replied with a smile that looked forced. "I had to move on, But hopefully I'll be back to stay soon."

Patrick was startled when the clock began to strike again. The chimes were beginning to sound more ominous. He was about to turn his head to look at it when Charlotte leaned across the table and pressed her soft lips against his. A warm tingling sensation spread throughout his body as he returned the kiss. For a moment Patrick felt the eyes of the crowd on him again, but at this moment he didn't care who looked. In that moment nothing mattered to him. The taste of Charlotte's lips made him dizzy with an ecstasy that he had only ever dreamed about. After what felt like an eternity Charlotte broke the kiss. Patrick let out a sigh of breath that he didn't even know that he had been holding. In the back of his mind the voice that had warned him

"Where did that come from?" Patrick when he caught his breath.

"I owed you a kiss from earlier." She replied as she sat back in her chair. "Besides, I wanted to thank you for calling me pretty." Patrick watched her cross her beautifully toned legs and smiled. Suddenly he knew that he couldn't let her just walk out of his life.

"What can I do to convince you not to go?" He reached out and cupped her hand in both of his own. This time Charlotte didn't pull back. Instead she squeezed his fingertips gently.

"It's a little more complicated than that." She replied after a moment. Her voice rang with a note of sadness that broke Patrick's heart to hear. "You don't know anything about me. I hate to use an old cliché, but you would hate me in the morning."

"Try me."

Charlotte smiled at him weakly and checked the little silver watch on her wrist. After a moment she looked back up at him and smiled.

"What do you say we get out of here?" She leaned forward in her chair.

"Are you sure?" he asked.

"Sure why not? The night is still young." Charlotte stood and offered Patrick her hands. He took them and got to his feet in turn. When he looked around Patrick noticed that everyone was still staring at him intensely. He hadn't noticed earlier because his mind was on Charlotte.

They started to make their way towards the door, but as they went Patrick noticed that the party guests were not moving out of their way as they had before. Instead people seemed to be trying to impede their movements. He would take a few steps in one direction only to be cut off by a small group. The voice in the back of Patrick's head screamed for him to try and force his way to the door, but there was no way he would be able to get through with Charlotte. Every route he could find was soon blocked off by another small group. In a matter of moments Charlotte and Patrick were surrounded by an angry looking crowd. Patrick instinctively stepped in front of Charlotte to keep himself between her and anyone meaning to do harm. The crowd slowly closed in on Patrick. He tried to watch everyone at once but they were able to keep him off balance.

Suddenly the grandfather clock chimed louder than it had before. The music stopped playing and the party guests all looked towards the clock. Both hands on the clock face pointed straight at twelve.

"One." Patrick heard Charlotte say behind him. Her voice had become distant and cold. The clock chimed a second time bringing a cold feeling into the pit of Patrick's stomach. He looked around to see all eyes had shifted from him to the clock.

"Two."

When the clock chimed for a third time Patrick's eyes grew hazy for a moment. His hands flew to his face and he rubbed at his eyes furiously. When he drew them away a horrified scream bubbled up from his throat. The crowd of party guests had all changed. What had until recently been a collection of attractive people had given way to so many rotting corpses.

"Three." Charlotte said behind him in a dry husk of a voice. Patrick turned around and screamed again. Charlotte was gone, in her place stood a dried out husk in a tattered red dress. The perfume that he had smelled was gone; instead his nostrils were filled with the scent of rotten meat. She reached out one bony hand towards Patrick's face and he swatted it away.

"I told you that you would hate me in the morning." The thing that had been Charlotte wheezed at him. The clock chimed again and Patrick heard someone in the crowd call out the number "Four." He pushed his way through the corpses as Charlotte followed him.

When the clock chimed a fifth time a murmur began to grow through the crowd. They were all waiting for something to happen but he was too busy pushing and shoving his way towards the door.

Christmas Spirits Rueckert

The sixth chime was accompanied by the sound of wood splintering. Despite his desire to escape Patrick spun around to see what had made the noise. What he saw almost stopped his heart dead. The Large black clock had disappeared. In its place he saw an enormous doorway filled with shimmering light. It was so bright that Patrick had to shield his eyes. Bony fingers closed over Patrick's arm and he spun to find himself face to face with Charlotte's rotting corpse. He tried to push her away but the hand tightened around his arm until he had to stifle a pained scream. Charlotte pulled him close to her with a worm eaten smile.

"The Gatekeeper is coming." She croaked. "And I won't go back alone." When the clock chimed for the seventh and eighth time the murmur in the crowd had become a roar. Patrick fought and clawed his way towards the door but the thing that had been Charlotte held fast to his arm. She tried to pull him towards the clock but he planted his feet and fought for every inch he could get.

When the clock chimed for the ninth time there was an icy blast of air and the crowd grew silent. Patrick peaked over his shoulder and saw the cause of the silence. In the middle of the doorway stood the figure of a man in a long hooded cloak. The figure looked around the room and spoke in a loud deep voice.

"Hear me souls of the dead. The time has come for you to return from whence you came. On the final stroke of midnight the gate will close. Transact what business you must in that time, for you shall then return to death."

Patrick's blood froze at the sound of the voice and He redoubled his efforts to reach the door. He clawed his way through rotting flesh and brittle bones until he finally laid his hand on the knob of the door.

"Stay with me Patrick." For a moment he could hear the sweet voice of the girl he had met before. The clock chimed again, was that ten or eleven? How many strikes left before the final? The thought gave strength to Patrick's efforts. He threw open the door and dove out into the night air. As he did he felt the bony hand wrapped around his wrist suddenly let go.

Christmas Spirits Rueckert

Patrick rolled over and looked back toward the entrance to the building just in time to see a bright flash. He sat there in the cold night air for what felt like an eternity. Off in the distance Patrick thought that he could hear a clock tower chime the final stroke of midnight. When he caught his breath Patrick stood up and inched his way towards the front door.

The door stood shakily on its hinges just as it had before. Patrick opened it shakily and looked inside and found the room surprisingly empty. There was no trace that there had been a party anywhere. The only thing that remained was the broken ruin of a burned out grandfather clock. Patrick turned his back on the empty building and walked down the street towards his apartment.

Do You Hear What I Hear?

"Sam, why did you agree to do this tonight of all nights?" Kyle asked as he adjusted the camcorder's aperture. When the picture on the view screen became clear he connected it to the rest of the system. "You had to pick the one night that I would rather be spending with my family and you drag me out here." Kyle stood up and set the camcorder on the tripod and aimed the lenses at the upper portion of the grand staircase. He checked the picture again and went back to the Table in the corner of the room that they had set up as a makeshift "command center".

Sam came up behind him and tussled his unruly hair. If she hadn't been Kyle's closest friend he would have told her to keep her hands to herself. But over the years he had become accustomed to her taking liberties. In another life the two might have become lovers, but the universe had other plans for the two investigators.

Christmas Spirits Rueckert

"I brought you here because this is the only night of the year that The Bloody Woman is supposed to materialize. Don't you think I would rather spend Christmas Eve with my own family? Now stop grumbling and help me finish setting up this equipment so we can go dark and get this show on the road."

Kyle sighed and went back to work. Sam was right; she had gone to a lot of trouble to get the permission of the owners of Blackthorn House to be allowed to conduct the hunt tonight. The house was usually rented out for the holiday season to local businesses as much as a year in advance. But this year news of the Christmas Eve hauntings seemed to have scared everyone away. Sam jumped at the chance to investigate one of the city's oldest historical homes. She claimed that she had convinced the owners that an investigation could alleviate any concerns about the hauntings. Kyle suspected that what really closed the deal was Sam's promise that the investigation wouldn't cost the owners anything. A sly smile spread across his face as he thought of this. If nothing else Sam knew how to get what she wanted.

Kyle hooked up the last few cameras in relative silence. Every now and then he would whisper words of encouragement to some of the older pieces of equipment to get it to cooperate. The total set up took almost two hours and the sun had set by the time he hooked up the last monitor.

"I am a genius!" he crowed when the monitors flickered to life in front of him. Sam just rolled her eyes.

"Tell me what you got Einstein." She joked as she sat down next to Kyle at the command station.

"Camera one is in the master bedroom where the employee's said they saw the mirror start to bleed. If you want my professional opinion that one is about as likely as me winning the Miss America pageant." Kyle took a moment co chuckle at his own joke; Sam just rolled her eyes again. "Camera two is in the Grand foyer aiming at the double doors that are supposed to open and close on their own." He indicated the monitor as he spoke. "Cameras Three Four and Five are aimed at three different angles of the Staircase that the Bloody Woman is supposed to appear on.

According to the legend that is where her jealous lover stabbed her to death back in the late 19th century." Sam looked at Kyle with genuine surprise.

"You really did your homework on this one. I'm impressed."

Kyle blushed a little; he had indeed done his homework. When Sam first told him that they would be investigating the Blackthorn house Kyle jumped headlong into the history of the house. Between in person interviews and old newspaper clippings he had learned everything he could about the house before he ever set foot inside. He had even gotten copies of the original blueprints and done a comprehensive study of them to see if there were any answers there.

"Now," Sam continued. "What do we have for audio?"

"Each camera has a microphone attached, I also have recorders set to activate at the slightest sound positioned in the kitchen and each of the guest bedrooms to pick up any EVP or other sounds we might encounter. I also rigged up a couple head mounted camcorders with built in microphones." Kevin pulled out a pair of devices that looked like a pair of headphones with a small webcam attached to one of the earpieces. "They connect to a hard drive you wear on your hip and the battery should last about four hours." He smiled as he hooked up one of the head cams to himself and offered the other to Sam.

"Someone's mood has improved." She smiled at him.

"Well you said it yourself; this is probably the only opportunity we'll get to capture the Bloody Woman on video." Kyle checked each camera one final time and then hit the main switch to kill the lights throughout the house.

Kyle took the first shift at the command station while Sam roamed throughout the old house. It was only eight thirty in the evening but the recent storm activity had covered many of the windows with snow and frost making the rooms darker than they would normally be. Kyle sat back in his chair and darted his eyes from one monitor to the next searching for any traces of movement. From time to time he checked the monitor that was picking up the feed from Sam's head cam. He smiled to himself when he saw how well the system was working.

Suddenly Kyle thought he saw a shadow move on the monitor for camera one. He leaned forward in his chair and watched even closer. The shadow shifted again and Kyle was about to grab his walkie talkie when he realized that it was probably just Sam walking around behind the camera. She had been gone for about fifteen minutes and had probably made her way into the master bedroom while he was checking the other screens. He looked to the screen that displayed Sam's head cam again but was shocked to see that she was investigating in the Grand Foyer. He shot his eyes back to the first monitor just in time to see it go dead. He grabbed for his walkie and thumbed the talk button.

"Sam, I'm going to run up and check the master bedroom. It looks like there is some activity and the camera just went out on me."

"What kind of activity?"

"I thought I saw movement just before the camera died, it could be nothing but I want to check it out anyway." Kyle stood up and made his way towards the grand staircase carefully avoiding the cords on the ground. He climbed to the second floor and made his way to the master bedroom. The room was decorated for Christmas with a tree in the corner and three little stockings on the fireplace. Kyle looked around for any source of the movement he saw on the monitor but found nothing ordinary that could explain it. Then Kyle decided that since he was in the room he would fix the camera and be on his way.

Kyle adjusted the cord to the camera and tightened the connection which must have gotten loose somehow because when it was back together the view screen on the camera flickered back to life. Kyle shook his head and decided to add it to the list of new equipment that they needed when he got back home. After one more sweep of the room to search for anything out of the ordinary Kyle walked out and started back down the stairs.

"Did you find anything?" Sam's voice crackled from the walkie on Kyle's belt.

"Nope, if this is all we have to look forward to, this is going to be a very long dull night." He said in response. The excitement he had felt earlier was beginning to diminish.

"Don't worry." The walkie chirped back. "Most of the weird stuff isn't supposed to happen for another two hours."

Kyle went back to the command center and sat down hard in his seat. Camera one was still operating and there didn't seem to be any problems with the other's just yet. Another quick check on Sam's head cam told him that she had left the foyer and was investigating in the kitchen. There were no concrete legends about that room but Sam was always as thorough when she investigated. That was one of the things that they had in common. With Kyle it was more about the research and the tech, but Sam would go into a place and look in every crack in the floorboards to try and find something that she could use.

After the first hour Sam returned to the command center and it was Kyle's turn to investigate the house. Since he had already been to the master bedroom Kyle decided to start his search in the kitchen where Sam had left off. The room was one of the only ones to have been remodeled in the modern style. It didn't quite fit with the house's old world charm. Instead stainless steel and tile covered almost every surface in the room. Kyle checked his instruments frequently but could find nothing in the kitchen that would even remotely be considered ghostly. Just as he was leaving the kitchen Kyle heard a loud thump coming from the ceiling just above his head.

"Did you hear that?" He asked into his walkie.

"Hear what?" Sam's disembodied voice replied from the black box.

"I just left the kitchen and I heard something fall on the floor right above my head."

"I didn't hear it but you should be right under the master bedroom. Let me check the monitor." During the moment of silence Kyle heard the same sound again. It was as though someone were bouncing a ball on the floor in exactly the same spot. "The monitor is clear Kyle. I don't see anything."

"I'll go back up and check then. It won't hurt just to make sure." Kyle said with a sigh.

The master bedroom had not changed since Kyle's earlier visit. The camera was still in place and the floor was free of foreign objects. He searched the room thoroughly but could find nothing capable of making the noise. When he was sure that there was no reason for the banging Kyle picked up the audio recorder and hit the playback button.

What he heard was a few seconds of dead air followed by the first thump. A smile spread across his face as he heard this. But the smile faded when the second thump didn't come. Instead there was a loud shriek on the recorder. He rewound and started it over and got the same response. One loud thump followed by a pained scream. After the second playing Kyle thumbed the record button and time stamped the clip for further investigation before returning it to the table where it sat.

Suddenly Kyle heard footsteps behind him. He turned around to see Sam standing in the doorway looking pale.

"What's wrong?" He asked.

"I heard someone coming down the steps." She said breathlessly. "At first I thought you were coming back down but then I saw you on the monitor. So I went to look and that's when I saw it."

"Saw what?"

"There was someone walking on the stairs, but it wasn't the Bloody Woman." Sam's eyes widened as she spoke. "It was a man in a black coat. I followed him but he disappeared at the top of the stairs." Kyle walked closer to Sam and put his hands on her shoulders reassuringly.

"Why does this have you so freaked out? You've seen ghosts before."

"This wasn't the same thing. Usually we just encounter residual hauntings. This one felt totally different. The man I followed, it felt like he was toying with me. He WANTED me to follow him. I had to find you and see what you found." She looked around the room and then back to Kyle. "Did you find anything?"

Kyle thought about playing the recording a third time but decided against it. Normally Sam would have been excited by seeing a possibly sentient apparition on an investigation. If she was already on edge then hearing that scream would probably do more harm than good. "I got some audio but I'd rather wait until I have more time to filter it before I say anything. I time stamped the anomaly. The air in the room was starting to feel heavy. At the same time he became aware of a familiar yet unpleasant aroma that he just couldn't place. Kyle looked around him and realized that the red light on the camera had gone out again. He quickly adjusted the cord and looked at Sam. "We should probably head to the staircase and see if we can get the apparition to contact us. Do you remember where it disappeared?"

Sam led Kyle to the top of the grand staircase and pointed to the center of the top step. "He got to the top step, made a half turn towards me and then vanished. I could still hear his footsteps going off towards the door to the master bedroom but those stopped about halfway down the hall. That's when I came to check on you. Something just didn't feel right."

Kyle got down on his hands and knees and leaned as far forward as he could. His face almost touched the top step. He took a deep breath through his nose and shuddered. "Sulfur, the steps smell like sulfur. That can't be a good sign." He pushed himself back up to a standing position and made a note of the time and location of the smell.

"I've never heard of a ghost smelling like sulfur." Sam said questioningly. "Most times if there is a recorded phantom smell it is ether cigar smoke or perfume." Kyle didn't know what to say. On top of her incredible people skills Sam was one of the best paranormal investigators he had ever met. Her only flaw came up when events didn't quite fall into the realms of her experience. If she couldn't reference a data bank to explain a phenomenon then she was lost on how to deal with it. Kyle's mind was teaming with thoughts but he had no way to express them clearly.

"I think there is more to this haunting than we originally thought." He finally said. It was clear that Sam wasn't sure exactly what he meant but before he could elaborate the doors in the grand foyer opened and slammed on their own. The sound echoed through the entire house startling the pair of investigators. Kyle went down the stairs two at a time and ran to the Command center to check the monitors.

Kyle checked Camera number one and saw nothing but snow. He thought about going back to fix it but decided to leave it be. All of the other monitors seemed to be in perfect working order. He looked up and saw Sam coming down the stairs slowly.

"Camera one crapped out on us again. The cords are shot so it's not worth the trouble to go up and fix it. I'll check camera two to see if we got anything when the doors slammed." He was already checking the hard drive as he spoke but Sam didn't seem to hear a word he was saying. Instead she walked into the middle of the room and cocked her head to one side as though she were listening for something. Kyle stopped what he was doing and approached her. "Are you alright Sam?"

Sam still didn't respond. She just kept staring off into space with a dreamy expression on her face. At length she came back to herself and looked bewilderedly at Kyle. "Don't you hear it?"

"I don't hear anything." He said flatly.

"I hear music." Sam said. Her voice took on a dreamlike quality that matched her expression. "It sounds like an orchestra." She started to sway back and forth to the rhythm of a song that only she could hear.

All at once Kyle heard something as well. But rather than spectral music played by a long dead orchestra Kyle was hearing footsteps coming down the stairs. He turned slowly in order to face whatever was coming. At first he couldn't see any source for the footsteps but as the sound descended a shape began to materialize. Each step brought the figure more solidly into view until at the last step Kyle found himself face to face with a young woman in a grey dress and veil. The Bloody Woman of Blackthorn house held her arms out to the investigator and he approached her spellbound.

Kyle began to hear the music that Sam had been talking about. It was a slow melodious waltz played by a string quartet. With every step he took Kyle could hear the music more clearly. When he stopped in front of her the ghost took him in her arms and the pair began to spin gracefully across the floor. Kyle lost himself in the dance. Every rotation across the floor brought him deeper into the ecstasy of the moment. He found himself wishing that the music would never end.

Suddenly the smell of sulfur invaded Kyle's nostrils and the spell was broken. When he looked at his dance partner what he had once seen as a beautiful woman gave way to a grinning skeleton. Kyle tried to push away from the Bloody Woman but the spirit's boney hands clung painfully to him. He fought as hard as he could until finally the spirit released its grip and fell to the floor in a clatter of bones.

Kyle ran to Sam's side and tried to shake her free of the spell but she was lost in the unearthly music. She tried to enfold him in her arms and dance with him but he would not let her. Over her shoulder Kyle caught another glimpse of the grand staircase. He was shocked to see a man in black standing at the top of the stairs where Sam had seen a similar figure disappear. The man in black was grinning at him wickedly. The sulfuric smell increased as Kyle looked at the figure. Rage boiled up inside the investigator and he stepped around his friend and approached the man in black.

"Who are you and what the hell have you done to my friend?" He demanded hoarsely. The man in black chuckled at him humorlessly before speaking.

"I am the true owner of this house young man." He said in a voice that sounded more animal than human. "And don't worry for the young lady. She will not be harmed, nor will she remember what happened this evening. She will awaken when the sun rises."

Kyle started up the steps towards the man in black with his hands balled up in fists. "You let her go right now you son of a bitch or I swear to God." He was cut off mid sentence by the sensation of a rope tightening around his throat.

"How dare you speak that way to me you filthy sack of meat?" The man in black spat in Kyle's face as the invisible rope tightened around his neck and lifted him from the ground. "You spend your time searching the strongholds of the dead for a glimpse of the life beyond. And when I come to show you that glimpse you treat me like some lowly wraith?"

Kyle reached his hand into his pocket for the small silver cross that he kept there but when he wrapped his fingers around it his hands froze in place. The man in black's eyes flashed with a fury that chilled the blood in his veins. Suddenly the pressure around Kyle's throat released and he dropped ten feet to the stairs. He didn't feel it when his body rolled down the steps breaking his neck. The last thing Kyle saw before the world went white was Sam swaying back and forth to Music that he could no longer hear.

When the caretaker came to check on the pair of investigators he was shocked at what he found. Sam sat in the corner crying over Kyle's body. The police investigated the incident but could find no traces of foul play. When they reviewed the tape from Kyle's head mounted camera the footage showed no anomalies. On the tape Kyle ran half way up the grand staircase and stops for a moment before falling. The official statement listed Kyle's death as an accident. Police reported that he must have slipped and fallen down the stairs in the darkness.

I'll Be Home for Christmas.

I had never picked up a hitchhiker before, but that night I felt like I had no choice. I was on my way home from a double shift on Christmas Eve when I saw him. The old guy looked like he had been walking for hours. His clothes were dirty and there was dried blood on the side of his head. When I drove past him he looked at me and I could see tears in his eyes. Something in the back of my mind told me not to stop but I couldn't just drive past without at least offering to help. I pulled over and flashed my headlights to get his attention. He walked up to the passenger side of the car and got in without saying a word.

"Where are you headed?" I asked after a few moments of silence.

"I need to get home. I promised my wife I'd always be home for Christmas." The old man replied in a tired voice. He looked like half frozen so I turned the heater up higher to let him get warm.

"Well I'll get you there on time. Just let me know where we're going." He gave me the directions and we pulled back onto the snow covered street. I looked over at my passenger again. He was holding a pocket watch in his hands and running his fingertips over the inscription. It was too dark for him to be able to read it but the look in his eye told me that he knew every word by heart. I smiled at him and nodded towards the time piece. "That's a nice watch, looks like one of the old fashioned ones you have to wind."

"It was a present from my wife the first Christmas we spent together. It has been in my pocket every day since she gave it to me." He said holding the watch by the chain so that I could see it better. "The engraving says 'Albert, this is to always remind you how precious the time we share is to me. Love always Your Annabelle."

"That's beautiful, and it's a pleasure to meet you Albert, My name is Mike Singer." I offered Albert one of my hands which he took. His fingers were so cold that it hurt my skin. When he let go I could still feel the icy impression on my hand.

"Albert Mclusky, but you can call me Al. Everyone else does." He smiled at me for the first time since he got in the car.

For the next fifteen minutes Al and I talked about our families. I told him about my wife and son and he told me everything about his wife Annabelle. They had met just before he was supposed to ship off to fight in Korea. He told me that he got wounded and was discharged from service just in time to make it back home for Christmas. Al's eyes practically sparkled when he talked about spending Christmas with Annabelle. It made me want to get home to my own family all the more.

My wife and I had been having a few problems lately. Mostly it was all of the overtime I put in at work to try and make Christmas a little easier. She kept saying that she didn't care if we had a big Christmas or not as long as we spent it together. I gave my passenger a sidelong look as I told him this. He was sitting quietly and shaking his head. His expression turned grave for a moment as he began to speak.

Christmas Spirits Rueckert

"Son, let me tell you something I learned a long time ago. Christmas isn't about who has the most presents under the biggest tree. You don't need the songs or the television specials or the food. What makes Christmas special is the time you spend with the people that care about you. Some of the most memorable Christmases Annabelle and I had were spent in a little two bedroom apartment where we sat up late looking at the lights on the tree and talking."

I sat quietly and let the old man's words sink in for a moment. He clapped me on the shoulder and pointed at a driveway just up the road. "That's my house; I can't thank you enough for picking me up. I was starting to think I'd never make it home."

"It was my pleasure Al. You gave me a lot to think about tonight. I think I'm going to go home and sit by the tree with my wife." He smiled at me and got out of the car. I watched him make his way up the walk towards the porch before I pulled out of the drive and headed home.

A smile spread across my face when I pulled into the driveway and saw the Christmas tree in the front window with all of the sparkling lights. When I opened the car door I noticed something shining in the passenger seat. I reached over and picked up Al's pocket watch. I thought about going back to give it to him but it was far too late at night for me to bother him at home. I decided I would return the watch to him in the morning. I went inside and told my wife all about the car ride. She looked a little worried at first when she heard that I had picked up a hitchhiker. But her worry turned into awe when I told her about Al just wanting to get home to his wife.

"You know what?" She asked with her eyes wide with excitement. "Since you're going to their house anyway we should invite Al and Annabelle over for Christmas dinner." I wrapped my arms around my wife and told her she was a genius. Al had told me that he and his wife didn't have much family in the area so it was perfect. I would drive back to Al's house the next morning after we opened presents and return the watch. When I was there I would invite he and his wife over for Christmas dinner.

My wife and I spent the rest of the evening sitting by the fire watching the lights on the tree sparkle and talking about our plans for the next day. In the morning we were awakened by my sun tearing through the house asking if it was time for presents. We spent the morning as a family and it was almost a shame when the time came for me to go deliver the watch.

It wasn't hard at all to find Al's house again. I walked up onto the front porch and knocked politely. After a few moments I heard the deadbolt slide and the door opened slightly. A small elderly woman looked out at me. I smiled pleasantly and nodded to her.

"Mrs. Mclusky I was wondering if I could speak to Al for a moment?"

The old woman looked at me as though I had just slapped her in the face. She stepped towards me with her finger pointed at my face. "Who are you? What do you want?" I took a step back and tried not to look threatening.

"My name is Mike Singer; I gave Al a ride home last night after his accident. He forgot his watch in my car and I just wanted to bring it back to him."

I pulled the watch from my coat pocket and showed it to the old woman. Her expression turned from one of anger to one of grief. She reached out and took the watch from my hand gently.

"Where did you find this young man?" She asked. I told her the story of the night before. How I had pulled over and gave her husband a ride home. I told her that he had talked about wanting to make it home to spend Christmas with her and that he had helped me realize that thanks to him I was more excited to spend the holiday with my own wife.

When I finished telling her my story Mrs. Mclusky invited me inside for a cup of coffee. I gladly accepted and asked her if Al had gone out to pick up his car. She just shook her head and walked over to a framed photograph on the mantle. She picked it up and showed it to me.

"Is this the man you drove here last night?" She asked. I looked at the picture and recognized Al instantly.

"Yup that's the man. He had me drop him off in the driveway, I watched him walk all the way to the door before I left. Didn't Al tell you all of this when he got home?"

Mrs. Mclusky looked at me evenly for a few seconds. After a while she appeared to come to a decision. She took the picture back and put it on the mantle. "Al never came home last night Mr. Singer; He hasn't been home in five years."

"But that's impossible; I dropped him off just outside the door. He told me he always spent Christmas with you."

"He always did Mr. Singer. Albert died in a car crash five years ago last night. He was on his way home from a business trip when his car went off a bridge into the river. I had told him not to rush but he told me that no matter what he would make it home for Christmas." A single tear fell from Mrs. Mclusky's eye. She took a moment to compose herself before she continued. She held up the watch that Al had left in the passenger seat of my car.

"My husband was buried with this watch in his hands Mr. Singer. He kept it with him ever since the day I gave it to him." She looked at the watch and held it out. "I think that he left it in your car because he wanted you to have it."

I stood dumbfounded for a moment. So many different emotions flowed through me at once. In one hand I was shocked at what Mrs. Mclusky was telling me, but on the other hand I remembered just how cold Al's hand was when we shook. After a moment I accepted the watch and put it in my pocket.

"Mrs. Mclusky I didn't just come over to give Al his watch back. It would be my pleasure if you would join my family for Christmas dinner tonight."

Mrs. Mclusky thought for a moment then a sweet smile spread across her face. She laughed slightly before she said, "Any friend of Al's is a friend of mine. I would be happy to accept Mr. Singer… but only on one condition."

"And that is?"

"Call me Annabelle."

Christmas Spirits Rueckert

That night Annabelle had dinner with my family and I. Deep down I think that Al would have been happy to know that she had someone to spend the holiday with. She even told our son a bedtime story when we tucked him in. Ever since that Christmas my wife and I are closer. We don't fight about money or how much time I spend at work. And I always make sure that I'm home for Christmas.

In the Bleak Midwinter

Christmas Spirits Rueckert

One of my fondest childhood memories was just sitting around the tree and listen to my grandfather tell stories of ghouls and ghosts. He would sit in his old chair and tell us about fantastic specters that he claimed to have encountered in his life. Some nights he would tell us about the ghost dog named spook that he claimed to keep in the basement to scare away burglars. Other times he would talk about his own version of the boogeyman. A terrifying spirit that he called the Boujok. Some of his stories scared me so badly that I couldn't sleep for days, but I loved every minute of it.

My grandfather always kept the best stories for special occasions. My favorite story that he ever told was on Christmas Eve when I was seven years old. We had just finished opening gifts and the room was a mess of colorful paper and boxes. My grandfather sat in his chair watching us play with our toys. Eventually he sat forward in his seat and smiled at us.

"Have I ever told you about the night I met a Banshee?" He asked with a smile.

"What is a Banshee?" My sister and I asked in unison.

"Not tonight Dad, it is Christmas Eve." My mom said in a serious voice, but her protest was buried under my sister and me cheering. He looked at her with his wicked smile and motioned for us to come closer so that we could hear his story.

"The Banshee is an ancient spirit from Ireland that foretells death." He held up a hand and pointed towards, a gesture that he was saying something important. "There are those who say that if you hear the Banshee keening, then you or someone you love will soon meet their death." I sat frozen by his words. My mother was about to protest again, but when she saw how my face lit up when my grandfather talked, she gave up and sat back on the couch.

"It all started on a Christmas Eve just like tonight." He said looking out the window at the snow. "I had just gotten off a double shift at the garage and was on my way home to spend the holidays with your mom and grandma. Two blocks away from the garage I see a woman standing in the middle of the road staring right at me. I had to swerve to avoid her, when I did my car hit a patch of ice and skid into a snow drift." My grandfather laughed and shook his head as he spoke. "I can tell you one thing; I was not using the most Christian language that night."

My mother cleared her throat and gave my grandfather the look that only a mother can master. In return, he smiled wickedly and continued.

"Anyways, there I was caught in a three foot high pile of snow. I rolled down the car window and shimmied out into the night air. When I got out onto the street I looked for the crazy lady who got her kicks out of standing in the middle of the road. I had a few things that I intended to say to her, but when I got to the spot where I had seen her standing the road was empty. I looked all around for fear that I might have clipped her when I swerved, but the only tracks I saw in the snow belonged to my old Chevy. Somehow a full grown woman had up and vanished like a puff of smoke. I decided that I must have imagined the whole thing. After all I had just come off a double shift and my eyes weren't what they used to be."

Christmas Spirits Rueckert

"I spent the next twenty minutes trying to dig the nose end of the Chevy out of the snow so that I could pull it into reverse. I had just about dug out the last tire when I heard the sound of a woman humming. It sounded like it was coming from right behind me", my grandfather hummed a few short notes, and it was a simple tune that I remembered hearing him hum before. "I looked over my shoulder to see who it could be, but there was no one else on the road that night. It was Christmas Eve and the whole town was either home or at midnight mass. I went back to digging my car out of the snow. It wasn't long before the humming started again, but this time when I turned around I was not alone. Standing behind me I saw a small woman in what looked like a white night dress. Her dark hair swirled in the wind like the tall grass in a field. I took a few steps closer and tried to get the woman's attention, but she just stood there swaying in the breeze while she hummed her sad low song. As I got closer she finally raised her head to look at me. When she saw me, her mouth spread in a wicked smile showing her sharp pointed teeth. I tried to take a few steps back but my feet slipped in the ice and I landed hard on my backside. That's when I noticed that the young woman's feet didn't touch the ground. Instead she sort of floated about an inch or two above it. My mother had told me stories from the old country since I was a child, so I knew right away that I was in trouble."

"How was she able to float above the ground Pop Pop?" The question came out without me even thinking. My grandfather laughed a little and looked down at me with a grin

"The Banshee is an old ghost; they have some crafty tricks up their sleeves my boy." My grandfather answered without missing a beat. "Mind what I say, never trust ghosts or faeries. If you do then you're done for."

"Don't fill his head with this nonsense." My mother scolded the old man with a smile. "And get back to the story. I want to hear what happens next."

"Like I said, The Banshee was just standing there grinning at me. I scrambled to my feet and looked around me for anything that would distract her from coming for me. She must have known what I was thinking because her song became louder. As she sang the Banshee slowly floated towards me still grinning her awful grin. Suddenly I remembered one of my mother's stories about the Banshee. She told me when I was young that the only way to stop a Banshee was at the point of a sword. I knew I didn't have a sword handy, but I decided to try the next best thing. I reached into the pocket of my work pants and pulled out my old buck knife. I flipped open the blade and pointed it straight at the Banshee's throat."

"Did it work?" I asked in a nervous voice.

"Well my boy I wouldn't be sitting here if it hadn't." He replied. "Now, do you want to hear the rest of this story?"

"Yes sir." I said eagerly

"Alright, then don't interrupt again or else we won't have time. It's getting late and I know Santa won't come until you're asleep in your own bed."

"Yes sir." I said again, this time with a hint of sadness.

"Ok then. There I was with the point of my old buck knife at the Banshee's throat. The singing had grown so loud now that it drowned out any other sound. I couldn't even hear the wind whistle in the trees. As soon at the Banshee touched the tip of my pocket knife she shot back three feet with an ear piercing wail. I held the blade firm in my hand and demanded to know what she wanted with me.

'Your time has come.' She sang to me in a soft voice that made the hand holding my knife feel weak. 'Tis your funeral dirge I sing Patrick O'Connor.' Hearing my own name made me clench the knife tighter in my hand.

'I won't be so easy to take,' I said as I took a step towards the Banshee with the knife. 'I ain't ready to go.' The Banshee floated outside my reach staring at the blade of my buck knife as though it were glowing hot. I thrust it towards her and she darted back until she was stuck between me and the back of my Chevy. When I had her trapped the Banshee let out another ear splitting scream and began to fade away. As she did, I heard her soft voice in the back of my head.

'You may have escaped me tonight. But I will be back for you Patrick O' Connor.'" My grandfather's face grew dark as he said this. For a long moment he just sat and looked out the window. "After that," he finally said. "I got back in my car and drove home. The next day when I went to clean my buck knife I noticed a green stain where the blade had touched the Banshee's throat. I must have scrubbed that blade with every cleaner known to man, but the green spot just wouldn't come off." With that he reached into his pocket and pulled out a battered old pocket knife. He opened the blade and showed it to me. Just as he had said, there was a green spot just on the tip of the blade.

That night on the way home my mother gave me the same speech that followed every one of Pop Pop's stories.

"You know you shouldn't believe everything your grandfather tells you. Right?"

"He showed me the green stain on his knife though." I said defensively.

"He probably used that knife to open a can of paint or something." She retorted. I couldn't see her face from the back seat but I could tell that she was rolling her eyes.

"Why would Pop Pop l lie to me?"

"It's not lying; your Grandfather just loves to tell stories. Some day you should ask him to tell the story about the day he kissed the Blarney stone." She said with a chuckle.

I don't remember what presents I got that year. I don't remember Christmas dinner, or what games we played at my cousin's house. The only thing that sticks out to me about that Christmas was my grandfather's story. In fact that story stuck with me for the next ten years.

Eventually I realized that my mother was probably right. My grandfather's stories were a lot of fun when I was little, but as I got older it became obvious that he was making it up as he went along. I still listened to his stories because I knew that he loved to tell them, but they had lost the magic that had made them so special.

That is, until one December night when I was seventeen. My grandfather had been sick for a few weeks, so I would visit him after school every day to make sure that he was doing alright. On the last day of school before break, there was a bad snow storm. School let out early so that everyone could make it home before the roads got too bad. I decided that I would go visit my grandfather early since I didn't know how bad the roads would get.

From the moment I walked into my grandfather's house I knew that something wasn't right. The air in the house felt thick and heavy in my lungs. I found my grandfather sitting in his favorite chair humming something to himself. The tune sounded familiar but I couldn't quite place it. I leaned over and placed my hand on the old man's forehead to check for a fever. The skin on his brow was cold and clammy. I tried a few times to snap him out of his reverie, but nothing seemed to work.

Finally I grabbed the phone from its cradle across the room and dialed 911. The phone on the other end rang twice before a female voice answered. I told her where I was and what was happening and she said that she would send paramedics right away and not to worry. Next I called my mother and told her what was happening. By the time I got off the phone I could hear the sound of approaching sirens.

The paramedics loaded my grandfather onto a stretcher and asked me if I wanted to accompany him to the hospital. I was about to say yes when I suddenly remembered why the song my grandfather was humming sounded so familiar. It was the same song that he told me the Banshee had been singing on Christmas Eve all those years ago. I told the paramedics that I would follow them, but I had to do something else first.

When the ambulance faded off into the snow I ran up the stairs to my grandfather's bedroom and threw open the top drawer of his bed side table. It took me a few minutes but I finally found what I was looking for. My grandfathers old buck knife was tucked away in a cigar box in the back of the drawer. I opened the blade and looked at it closely. There was a dark green stain on the tip of the blade. I stuffed it into my pocket and ran out into the storm.

Christmas Spirits Rueckert

The snow was coming down in sheets and I could barely see past my windshield by the time I got on the road. Turning on the headlights just made things worse because it just made the white snow that much brighter. The only things that would cut through the snow were the fog lights. Luckily the streets were all but deserted due to the storm.

Suddenly just ahead of me I saw the outline of a human in the snow. Someone was standing in the middle of the street. I had to cut my steering wheel hard to the right to avoid hitting them head on. When I did my car stalled out just inches away from a telephone pole.

I threw open the door to my car and jumped out to check to make sure that I hadn't hurt anyone. When I did I saw a woman in what appeared to be a white nightgown standing just in front of me. Her long dark hair swirled in the wind like the tall grass in a field. My grandfather's description of the Banshee flashed into my memory. I took a step closer and could just barely hear the sound of her humming to herself amid the storm. My heart skipped a beat and I immediately reached for my grandfather's pocket knife. But before I could touch the handle the Banshee let out an ear splitting

cry that brought me to my knees.

Slowly she floated towards me and grinned. I saw the

mouth full of sharp teeth that my grandfather had told me about so

many years before. I reached for the knife again but the Banshee

held out her hand and I froze in place. Her voice came to me

clearly through the noise of the storm.

"Do not be afraid young man." She sang in a voice so

sweet that I almost began to cry. "This is not the night that I come

for you."

"Then why are you here?" I demanded. Once again I tried

for the knife, but my hand would no longer move.

"I have come to collect a debt from Patrick O'Connor. His

time has once again come."

"I won't let you take him." I yelled, but my voice was lost

in the wind.

"Dear child. Do not think that you could stop me if you wanted to." The voice came again. This time I could feel the words resonating in my mind. Suddenly a figure walked up alongside the Banshee. As it got closer I could make out the details of the figure. It was tall man wearing work pants and a long sleeve button down flannel shirt. When he came close enough I could recognize my grandfather's face. He knelt down in front of me with a smile. For a moment the sounds of the storm all died away. All that I could hear was the beautiful melody of the Banshee's song.

"Don't worry about me boy, I'm ready to go this time." He said calmly. "I've had a good life. Now it's time I see what's beyond." My grandfather put his hands on my shoulders for a moment before he stood up and turned towards the Banshee.

In an instant they both vanished into the storm. I sat there alone for a moment before I turned and got back into my car. I turned the key and the engine roared back to life.

When I got to the hospital my mother was waiting for me in the lobby. She threw her arms around my neck and cried into my shoulder. Then she took a step back and looked me in the face.

"Your Grandfather is."

" I know." I interrupted her. "He didn't make it."

"What happened to you?" she asked. "I thought that you were going to ride with the ambulance."

"You wouldn't believe me if I told you." I answered as calmly as I could. She looked at me questioningly but decided not to press the matter.

When we got home that night I went to my room and pulled out my grandfather's buck knife. I opened the blade and inspected it closely. I took my thumbnail and scraped at the side of the stain but nothing happened. I thought back to the events of the day and sighed. I knew that no one would believe me if I told them what had happened. But it would be one hell of a story to tell my grandchildren some day.

Little Drummer boy

I sat at the kitchen table and watched the scruffy faced technician set up his equipment. "We have a clip we would like you to hear." he said as he adjusted the volume knob on the speaker system. When he had achieved the level he wanted he tapped a key on his netbook computer. The silence was broken by the sound of a drum roll followed by a distinctly militaristic sounding drum cadence. The sound of drumming continued for a few seconds before the room once again faded into silence. "Is this the same sound you reported to us?"

"Of course it is," I replied impatiently. The drumming was exactly like I had heard almost every night since I moved into my house three weeks ago. It had started out as a faint tapping, but over time the sound grew steadily over time. I told myself that it was just water in the pipes, or the sound of the house settling. As it grew more distinct I realized that there was something supernatural behind the drumming. Sometimes the sound seemed to come from another room, others it was like the drummer was right behind me. Eventually the noise became too much for me to live with.

Christmas Spirits Rueckert

I tried everything I could think of to try and get rid of the sound. At first I tried to sleep with noise canceling headphones, but the sound just got louder. I even went so far as to ask my sister's pastor to do a blessing on the house, but nothing worked. Every night I still woke to the beat of an unseen drum. There was no way that I could move out. I had spent more than half of my savings on this house and after the blessing failed; my sister suggested that I try to find the source of the phenomenon. She said that if I could pinpoint exactly what was causing the phantom drumming then it would be easier to deal with. She gave me the number of a local paranormal investigator. Her name was Samantha Alvarez and she was supposed to be the best investigator in the area. It didn't take long to convince me that this was the right course of action. I called her and set up an interview a few days later.

Samantha met me at a small coffee shop downtown and I told her all about the drumming. She took notes on a legal pad as we talked and she asked me if I would be alright with her and her partner conducting an investigation in my home. I told her that if it would get rid of the noise that I would let them do whatever they felt they needed to. She promised me that the investigation would be discrete and professional.

The next time I met Samantha was the night of the investigation. She introduced me to her partner Kyle. After we exchanged pleasantries I gave them a guided tour through the house and told them everything I knew about its history. All I knew is what the real estate broker had told me when he showed me the house. The last tenants were an elderly couple that had to move out after a few months due to money troubles. He wouldn't tell me anything else about the previous tenants.

"Can you tell us where the majority of the activity takes place?" Samantha asked when we had finished the main floor of the house.

"Honestly, I don't think there is a room in the house that I haven't heard the drumming. Sometimes it even follows me from room to room." Samantha scribbled furiously on her legal pad for a moment then looked back up at me.

"Have you done any renovation since you moved into the house?" Kyle asked in his turn. I told him that aside from a fresh coat of paint and rearranging some furniture, I hadn't changed a thing.

"Besides," I continued. "I didn't need to change much since most of the house had to be rebuilt about ten years ago."

"Why was the house rebuilt?"

"There was a fire that almost completely destroyed the place. All that was left was the basement and part of the first floor." Samantha took some more notes and we pressed on.

I lead the way to the second floor and pointed out the places where the sound seemed to be the loudest. Kyle marked a few spots with electrical tape as we went. The final stop on our tour was in the basement. Sam asked me about any activity and I told her that the basement is where I had first heard the drumming. She broke away from us and started to inspect the walls and floor of the basement more thoroughly. Kyle must have been tired of just watching, because he began to search things on his own. After a few minutes, Samantha called me over to one of the corners of the basement. When I got there she pointed her flashlight along the edge of the wall."

"Do you notice anything out of place?" She asked quietly as though she didn't want to draw too much attention to herself. I looked closer and realized that the bricks looked funny.

"The bricks along this section of wall seem to be out of alignment. It looks like someone took down a portion of the wall and re bricked it."

"Why would anyone do that?"

"I don't know," I answered. "Maybe there was a problem with the masonry and they had to fix it quickly."

"We will have to look into that when we conduct our investigation." Samantha replied after a moment's silence.

When the two ghost hunters had finished their cursory inspection of the basement I lead them back upstairs and left them to their investigation. We had decided that I would spend the night in a hotel to avoid tainting any of their experiments. I must admit

that I the prospect of a night of uninterrupted sleep made it easier

to assent.

By the time I got back home the next morning the

investigators had already left. I pulled out my phone and dialed

Samantha's cell number. The phone rang twice before she

answered.

"Hello?" The voice on the other end sounded far away. I

could hear the clicking of a computer keyboard in the background.

It was obvious that I was on speaker phone.

"Hi Samantha, I was calling about the investigation last

night. How did everything go?" When I finished I heard a distinct

rustling noise on the other end followed by a beep. When

Samantha spoke again her voice was loud and clear.

"We got several hours worth of footage." She still sounded

a little preoccupied. "I'm actually going over some right now.

There are a few things you will probably want to see. Give us a

couple of days and we will be able to sit down and show you what we have." I told her I looked forward to hearing from her and ended the call.

I spent the rest of the day wondering what kind of footage the investigators could have captured. When Samantha had agreed to investigate my claims I had expected them to capture some audio of the drumming, but it had never occurred to me that there might be some kind of picture to go along with it. A chill ran up my spine when I thought about what they might have to show me.

That night I was sitting at the kitchen table eating dinner when the drumming started. Just as it had so many other nights, the rolling cadence beat in my ears for a few moments before it began to move off into the distance. Finally I had had enough. After trying so hard to ignore the sound I decided to track the it to its source.

I rose from my chair and followed the phantom drummer through the house. Each time I thought I was making progress the beat would stop only to start again in another room. Frustrated, I would change direction and try to catch up to the disembodied sound. I wandered the house like a man possessed. The only thought in my mind was to follow the drum beat wherever it might lead me. Finally I tracked the sound to the door that leads to the basement. A feeling of pride swelled in my chest. I had the thing cornered; there was nowhere to run to anymore. I seized the door and threw it open with a cheer of triumph.

When the door opened a cold blast of air cut through my body. The feeling caught me by surprise and I lost my balance. I tried to steady myself by holding onto the doorknob, but my hand slipped and I fell to the floor with a loud thud. As I lay there for a moment the sheer stupidity of my actions struck me and I began to laugh at myself. I laughed so hard that my eyes filled up with tears that began to run down my cheeks.

Eventually I found my composure and stood back up. I did a quick check to make sure that the only thing bruised was my pride. Then I shut the closet door and walked back downstairs to the kitchen. I spent the rest of the evening sitting quietly waiting for the drumming to start again. When nothing happened after several hours I went to bed and slept uneasily.

The next morning I woke up to the ringing of my telephone. I answered it on the last ring before the voicemail picked up the call.

"Hello?" I said with a yawn.

"Hey Tom, this is Kyle Mclusky. You might not remember me but I work with Samantha. I just finished compiling the footage from the other night and was wondering if you would be available to meet with me today?"

"I thought Samantha was handling my case."

"Something came up at the last minute and she asked me to handle the meeting for her." He said in a voice that sounded slightly annoyed. I told Kyle that I would be free all day and that he could come over whenever he had the opportunity. Two hours later we sat in the kitchen listening to a perfect recording of the phantom drumming.

When the recording faded out Kyle asked me if that was the exact drumming I had heard. My answer didn't seem to shock him in the least. "I was just making sure," he said with a tired smile. "To be honest, I had no trouble finding this clip. I was standing by the recorder when it started. It was so loud that it sounded like someone was standing right behind me beating on a snare. The only problem with that is that I was alone in the house at the time."

"Where was Samantha?" I asked.

"We take turns investigating on our own while the other one watches the monitors. There are at least two more clips from when Sam was investigating but this one was the best." Kyle looked from me to the audio recorder with a proud smile.

"Samantha said she wanted me to see something?" as soon as the words left my mouth I began to regret saying them. Kyle must have sensed my discomfort because his smile grew.

"Don't worry; we didn't get any video evidence. I wish we had, but this one seems to be a strictly audible haunting." As he spoke Kyle closed the computer and picked up a manila envelope. He opened the envelope and handed me a few photos and a newspaper clipping. "Sam wanted to show you these herself, but she's trying to negotiate a deal with the owners of Rosewood house so that we can investigate on Christmas Eve."

"Isn't Rosewood house the place downtown that's supposed to be the most haunted house in the state?"Kyle rolled his eyes before he responded.

"Yeah, This is the first year that they aren't booked solid through New Years so Sam wants to drag me out on Christmas Eve to give the place a once over. Sam thinks it's a big deal but I would honestly rather not talk about it." Kyle shook his head and looked back to the photos in my hand. "Anyway, Sam did some research on your house to try and figure out who or what could be haunting it As it turns out, part of your property belonged to an old confederate family during the civil war. The youngest boy must have been the black sheep of the family, because he joined the union army as a musician. I'll give you three guesses what instrument he played."

"He was a drummer." I said confidently.

"Right on the first try." He pointed at one of the photos and I picked it up. It was a picture of a union battalion. In the front row of the picture was a sixteen year old boy kneeling off to the side. There was a snare drum dangling from a strap across his shoulder. Kyle tapped the photo with the tip of his finger as he spoke. "The kid goes through the whole war without suffering from so much as a cold. His older brother wasn't so lucky. He was caught bushwhacking and the Union army hanged him for treason. I guess the kid wasn't too happy about his brother being killed, because he apparently deserted and ran back to his family. The army followed him back to his home town, but after that he seems to have just disappeared."

"What do you mean disappeared?"

"Nobody knows what happened to him, one day he comes back from the war and the next he just up and vanishes. Some of the townspeople swore that they saw him around town in uniform, but his parents said that they hadn't seen him. The only thing suggesting that he made it home was a report from one of the neighbors. He said that the day the boy came home he heard the sound of a struggle in the house. Eventually he was just listed as a deserter and the army just gave up looking."

I took in everything that Kyle told me and processed it for a minute. Deep down I knew that the boy had made it home. That was the only explanation for the phantom drumming. "Maybe he did make it home, but he didn't get the warm welcome he expected."

"What do you mean?"

"I mean that the kid's parents killed him. Either by accident or intentionally and they hid his body in the house to cover it up." I got up from my chair and went to the basement door. After a moment Kyle got up and followed me.

We went down to the basement and I handed Kyle a crow bar from my work bench. Then I led him to the section of wall that Samantha had pointed out to me a few days before. In a matter of minutes we broke a hole in the section of wall with the crowbar.

Buried in the hole in the was a skeleton wrapped in the rags of an old Military uniform with the handle of a rusted knife sticking out of the ribcage. The skeleton held a snare drum wrapped in its bony arms.

When we cleared out the rest of the opening I called the police to let them know what we had found. A few days later I stood alone in the cemetery and watched the city workers bury the remains of the young soldier. When they finished I stood for a long moment looking at the grave and listening for the sound of drums off in the distance, but the air was silent.

No Room at the Inn

"I'm sorry," the old woman behind the counter said. "All of our available rooms are occupied."

"You've got to be kidding me." Alex said with a sigh. He gestured towards the window and the blizzard outside. The snow fell in thick flakes that swirled in the wind. "I can't go back out there. The roads are buried and there is zero visibility. I was lucky that I got here in one piece. Are you sure there's nothing? I don't care if I have to sleep on a couch."

He studied the old woman's face for a moment, but there was no sign that his appeals were having any effect. She just looked from him to the hotel register. The storm must have been a heaven sent for the small inn. Everyone that had been traveling when the snow hit was forced to take shelter or risk getting stuck in the storm. This was the third one in twenty miles that he had tried. Everyone had told him that they had just rented out the last room available. Alex thought about trying one last appeal but the old woman held firm.

"Fine," he said in an exasperated voice. "I'll try and find something else farther down the road." He turned to leave but the old woman reached out and touched his arm.

"Wait, this is the last place for at least thirty miles. The way that storm is coming in you wouldn't make it more than ten." She said with concern in her voice. For a second Alex thought he saw fear in the old woman's face. She shifted uncomfortably behind the counter and looked at him seriously. "We do have one more room." Her face colored a little when she said this. Alex stared at her dumbfounded for a second.

"Then why did you try to tell me that you were full up?" He tried to hide the agitation in his voice.

"We haven't rented it out in years." The color drained out of the old woman's face as she reached under the counter and pulled out an old battered key. "The room is in the attic, so we don't get many people wanting to use it. We've been using it for storage, so it's a little cluttered."

"I wouldn't care if I was sleeping on one of your dining room tables. Anything is better than spending the night in the back seat of my car." He replied as he pulled off his gloves and went searching for his wallet. "How much is it for the night?"

"No charge." She held out the key to Alex with a forced smile.

"I couldn't take a room without paying for it. It wouldn't be fair"

"I insist. That old room isn't worth what we would charge for it. " Alex reluctantly took the key and smiled at the old woman. "Do you need me to have someone get your bags?" She asked. Alex shook his head and pointed to the overstuffed backpack that was slung over his shoulder.

"I'm all set. How do I get up to the room?"

"I'll take you up. The bed is going to need fresh linen's if you'll be sleeping up there." The old woman disappeared into a back room for a moment and returned with a fresh set of sheets. Alex followed her through the house to a large spiral staircase. The Inn was well maintained. It was obvious that someone had gone to great lengths to keep everything in running order. The old woman led Alex up a flight of stairs to the second floor. Then she turned a corner and led him down a long hallway.

When they got to the end of the hall Alex noticed a painting that looked out of place with the houses cheerful ambiance. It was a portrait of a stern looking woman in a black dress. Her salt and pepper hair was pulled into a tight bun that made her age difficult to guess. The woman could have been anywhere from thirty to sixty. She was seated in a large wing back chair and holding an ornate silver cane in her hands. She also wore a silver charm on a chain around her neck. Somehow it looked familiar to Alex, but he couldn't figure out how. It looked like a small number eight turned on its side. He found himself being drawn to the painting;

something about it seemed to call to him. At the same time just looking at the woman's face made Alex uncomfortable.

"What do you think of Head Mistress DelMonica?" The old woman said from behind Alex. The sound of her voice made him jump. He turned and smiled at her. "Isn't she just as lovely as a rose blossom?" There was a trace of irony in the old woman's voice as she said this.

"Who is she?" he asked.

"She was one of the original owners of the house. Back in the nineteenth century this house was a school for girls. Head Mistress DelMonica was in charge for almost twenty years before she passed away." The old woman looked up at the painting and shuddered.

"I wouldn't want to be on her bad side. Just looking at it makes me feel like someone is walking on my grave." A cold feeling spread up my spine as I continued to look at the painting.

"I'm sure she wasn't all bad. But I hate that painting. Sometimes when I'm cleaning the halls I swear I can feel her watching me. It's like after all these years she still wants the place to be run her way." The old woman shuddered again and continued walking. After a few paces Alex followed.

"Why do you keep the painting up if you obviously don't like it?" Alex asked the old woman. She replied with a timid laugh.

"I would love to get rid of the hideous thing, but its part of the history of the town. You can't just tear down a piece of history. It's just not done around here." The tone of her voice told Alex that there was no more room for discussion.

The old woman lead Alex up one final flight of stairs and stopped just outside a locked door.

"Here you are," she said with the same forced smile that Alex had noticed earlier. "Just let me open the door and we'll get you all settled."

Alex pulled the battered key out of his pocket and slid it into the lock. When he turned the key it moved smoothly as if it had been used just that morning. The old woman walked into the room and threw a switch on the side of the wall. The overhead lighting blinked to life. The inside of the room was filled with random stacks of boxes and things. A queen sized four post bed sat in the middle of the room. It was obvious that no one had slept in this room in quite a long time.

Alex pulled one of the dust covers off of a large dressing table and looked closely. The craftsmanship of the piece was amazing. Someone had taken great pains to hand carve the figures on the desk. He looked around the room and noticed that among the boxes were several other pieces of furniture hidden beneath old sheets.

"This room is huge." he said as he looked around.

"It's the biggest room that we have." She looked around at the room. "It's also the hardest to rent, we had to just converting it into storage space."

"Why did you stop renting it out?" He asked as he watched the old woman making the bed.

"Oh, you know how it is. An old house like this has to settle on itself every now and then. When it does some young folks get funny ideas in their heads." She answered as she adjusted the fitted sheet to the mattress.

"What kinds of Ideas?"

"It's nothing you need to worry about young man. I wouldn't want you getting all worked up about nothing." She laid the pillows that she had brought with her on the mattress and smoothed out the wrinkles with practiced ease. It was obvious that there was something that she wasn't saying, but Alex didn't even know what questions to ask. As soon as the bed was made and the old woman stood up and started towards the door. She stopped with her hand on the knob and looked back at Alex. "Dinner will be served in an hour and a half," she said before she turned around and closed the door behind her.

When Alex was alone he looked around the room again. The air was thick and dusty, but overall the room was still just a room. The wooden floors were almost entirely covered by a large area rug to keep his footsteps from echoing when he walked across the room. Alex found a chair in the corner of the room and dropped his backpack on it. The bag blew up a small cloud of dust when it struck the cushion. He stood there for a moment thinking about why the old lady had made such a fuss about the room. It was obvious that she had been lying about the difficulty in renting the room. A few noises here and there could be easily covered up. With a little work this room could easily bring in a couple hundred dollars per night.

Outside the snow continued to cover the ground in a thick white blanket. Alex looked out the window of his attic room and watched it swirl and dance through the sky as it fell. He stood there for a moment and thanked his lucky stars that he had been able to find someplace to stay for the night. If he had tried to sleep in his car he was sure he would have frozen to death.

Suddenly Alex thought that he heard footsteps behind him. He slowly turned, expecting to see the old woman coming in the door to retrieve something that she forgot. Instead he found himself looking at an empty room. He reminded himself what the old woman had told him about the house settling. All of the wind and snow blowing across the rooftop of the house must have been making the beams shift. Alex felt a cold wind on the back of his neck and shivered slightly. "The wind must have blown in from a loose shingle, but I can see why people would get the wrong Idea." He said to himself as he pulled his coat closer around him to ward off the cold. He would ask the owners for an extra blanket for the night.

Alex went down to dinner half an hour before it was supposed to be ready. On his way down the stairs he stopped by the painting of Head Mistress DelMonica again. Just like before, the woman in the painting scowled back at him. Somehow the look of the portrait made Alex more uncomfortable than before. Something about the woman's piercing eyes made him feel as though they were watching him. He turned his back on the display and went the rest of the way downstairs.

When he got to the main dining room Alex sat down close to the fire place and watched the flames dance for a while. He gradually became aware that there was someone in the seat next to his. He looked up and saw a middle aged man wearing a colorful sweater watching him. A welcoming grin spread across his rounded face. When Alex looked up the man offered him his hand.

"Hey there stranger, my name is Carl Fuller. What brings you to the Fairfield Inn?"

"Hey there Carl," he replied as he took Carl's hand and shook it politely. "My name is Alex. I got caught in the snow and needed a place to stay for the night." Carl laughed and clapped the young man on the shoulder.

"Aint that the truth. I might be the only person here tonight who wasn't knocked off the road because of this blizzard." Carl laughed at his own comment. For the next twenty minutes Carl and Alex discussed the various occupants of the Inn. First Carl told Alex about the elderly couple that owned the place. Their names were Peg and Andrew Fairfield and they had bought the building twenty years before and had run the place ever since.

Most of the current guests were vacationers that were trapped by the snow. Carl was one of only five guests who had booked their trip to the Fairfield intentionally.

"I'm here working on researching local legends about witchcraft for a book I'm writing." He said without a trace of concern who heard him. "This town was booming when the spiritual movement of the late nineteenth century took off." Carl was about to give some examples when Mrs. Fairfield came out to announce dinner. The two men found a table in the corner of the room and sat together waiting for the meal to be served.

"So, what room are you in Alex? I don't think I saw you come in." Carl asked between bites of turkey and mashed potatoes.

"Oh, I was the last one here so I got stuck with the room in the attic." Carl's jaw dropped open and the color drained from his face. Alex looked at him questioningly but the older man was silent for a long moment.

"You got the Head Mistress's room?" He said finally. "Man, you are braver than I am. I can tell you that without a doubt."

"Why do you say that?" Alex asked. The look on Carl's face worried him a little.

"You haven't heard the stories?"

"No, what stories are you talking about? Mrs. Fairfield told me that it was hard to rent out the attic room because of all of the noises of the house settling at night."

Carl shook his head and looked Alex in the face. "The noise aint the problem. One of the last people to stay in that room was a banker. He checked in for a night and when they found him the next day he was hanging from the rafters. Police called it a suicide but some of the locals have their own Idea."

"Like what? Do they think he was murdered?"

"Have you seen the painting of the old head mistress up on the second floor?"

"Yeah, she doesn't look like she would be much fun at a party." Alex smiled for a second but stopped when he noticed that his joke hadn't had the desired effect on the older man. Carl looked around the room to make sure no one else was listening before motioning for Alex to lean closer.

"According to the rumors, the banker killed himself because he couldn't stand to stay another night in that room. He kept staring at the painting and mumbling to himself."

"So the painting drove him loopy?" Alex asked with a grin. "What does that have to do with anything? I thought you were researching witches? Not ghost stories."

"I have research that shows that Head Mistress DelMonica was a witch." He said in a voice so low that Alex had to strain to hear him.

"What?" Alex asked. "You mean she was part of the spiritual movement you were talking about?"

"Worse than that." Carl said as he leaned closer "There are stories that she performed black magic up there. The old folks say that she was trying to make herself immortal. Obviously she didn't succeed, but most people around here believe that her spirit haunts the Fairfield. I even hear tell that her spirit is trapped in that painting."

Alex spent the rest of the meal dwelling on what Carl had just told him. If any of this was true then he understood why the Fairfield's were so reluctant to rent out the attic room. At first he thought Carl was just pulling his leg. In the short time he had talked to the man it was obvious that Carl was a man who enjoyed a good joke. Eventually he decided that the only way he could be sure was to ask the Fairfield's.

He found the old couple seated at the head of a large table. The old woman smiled when she saw him approach.

"How are you enjoying your stay so far?" She asked in a cheerful voice that made Alex slightly uneasy. Especially after her obvious discomfort when she accompanied him to his room.

"Everything is beautiful but I had a few questions to ask you about my room if you have a moment."

The Fairfield's looked at each other and then back to Alex. After a moment Mr. Fairfield rose from his seat and the two men walked to the main lobby. When they got there the older man closed the doors to the dining room and turned to look Alex in the face.

"What can I do for you son?" He asked in a fatherly tone.

"I just had a question about my room if that's alright?"

"We have so many guests tonight. I hope you wouldn't mind reminding me what room we set you up in." Mr. Fairfield knew very well which room Alex was staying in. He was just trying to guide the conversation to some point, but Alex didn't know what.

"When I checked in this afternoon your wife gave me the room in the attic." All of the blood ran from the old man's face. A split second later Mr. Fairfield composed himself and smiled. If Alex hadn't been expecting some kind of reaction he might have missed it entirely.

"Yes, I remember now. You were the young man that my wife made room for in the storage space." The old man clapped his hand on Alex's shoulder and laughed. "How are you faring up there?"

"Your wife said that you used to rent that room out." Alex pointed out.

"Oh Heavens no. for a while we had considered converting it into a sort of honeymoon sweet," the old man said. "In the end it just ended up costing too much to finish. Now we keep it for emergencies. Take tonight for example; if we hadn't kept that room empty then you might still be stranded out on the road somewhere." The old man forced a laugh and started to turn back towards the dining room when Alex caught him by the elbow.

"Is my room haunted?" Mr. Fairfield froze in place for a moment before turning back to the young man.

"You've been talking to Carl haven't you?" He asked with an smug smile. .

"We might have discussed a thing or two." Alex shot back with his face stern.

"I wouldn't be too worried about anything Carl has to say. He spends so much of his time looking for ghoulies and ghosties and long legged beasties that he probably sees them everywhere he turns these days. There are no ghosts in the Fairfield Inn. Even if there were I don't see how you have much room to complain. My wife isn't charging you for the night's stay in your room if memory serves." Alex tried to think of a retort, but words failed him. After he said his piece the old man went back to the dining room and sat down with his wife.

Alex knew right away that the old man was lying. He wouldn't have brought up the topic of money if he wasn't trying to hide something. Alex walked back into the dining room and pulled up the chair next to Carl.

"Let me guess." The older man said with a tired smile. "He just gave you the brush off didn't he?"

"Only after he said that you have ghosts on the brain." The stupidity of the situation made Alex chuckle. Before long Carl joined in. After the stress of the day it felt good to let off a little pressure. They laughed together for a while, and then Carl put his hand on the younger man's shoulders with a smile.

"You wanna stay the night in my room? I've got an extra bed."

"No thanks," Alex replied. "I think I'm just gonna go upstairs and crash. After the day I've had I doubt anything could wake me up. If I'm wrong then who knows? I've never met a real live ghost before." He was about to start laughing again, but stifled it when he saw the grim expression on the older man's face.

"Alright, but I'm staying in room number twenty three if you change your mind." Carl stood up and shook Alex's hand before leaving the dining area. One by one the other guests made their way upstairs leaving Alex alone with his thoughts. He sat quietly staring at what was left of the fire while the Fairfield's and their employee's cleaned up the dining room. Eventually they finished their work and left as well. As they went the Fairfield's turned down the lights and Alex sat alone in the dark.

For a while he considered just sleeping on the nearest couch and just make the excuse that he must have dozed off while reading if anyone found him. It was the thought of a big queen sized bed all to himself that finally convinced Alex that he would be better off going back to his room for the night. After all, he still wasn't sure that the room really was haunted.

When he passed the Head Mistress's portrait Alex made a point to look in the other direction. Even though he refused to look at it he still felt uneasy just knowing that it was there. It was like the eyes of the woman in the painting were staring right at him. Alex unconsciously quickened his pace as he walked up the final flight of stairs to the Attic.

It was easy for Alex to be brave when he was in a room full of people. But as he entered the Attic a cold fear bubbled in the pit of his stomach. Alex looked around the empty room with a feeling of amazement. Nothing had changed at all since he went down to dinner almost four hours before. Everything was exactly as it had been. But somehow the room felt different. There was a menacing quality to the room as a whole that made Alex's skin crawl. Every creak of wood made him jump. Out of the corner of his eye Alex thought he saw a shadowy figure swaying from the rafters. No doubt the body of the man who committed suicide. He suddenly remembered how quickly the old woman had left the room after making the bed. It was as though she couldn't wait to get back downstairs.

Alex tried to shrug off the feelings of unease. He kept reminding himself that he was better off inside than he would have been on the road. The snowstorm had gotten even worse since he checked in and there was talk among the other guests of a level three emergency. That would mean that he would be stuck here for at least another night. If that was the case then he might take Carl up on his offer to share rooms. One night in this room would be more than enough.

Slowly Alex was able to push the negative feelings about the room out of his mind. Nothing had happened to make him believe that the Fairfield Inn was haunted. The owners may have acted a little strange at times, but that could just be a result of the high stress situation. After all, the Inn did fill up rather quickly when the storm started.

Over time the uneasiness melted away into exhaustion and Alex decided to go to bed. He lay down on the mattress and pulled the blankets up to his chin to ward off the cold night air. It wasn't long before his eyelids became heavy and he fell into a deep sleep.

That night Alex dreamt that he was in the dining room of the Fairfield Inn. He was sitting in the same corner table that he had shared with Carl the night before. But somehow everything in the room was different. He looked around at the other guests only to realize that they were all staring at him. He could feel dozens of eyes burning into him at every point. Then the crowd parted and Alex saw the woman from the painting come walking towards him.

She looked younger and more beautiful than she had in the painting. The streaks of grey hair that had speckled her head were gone. In their place were long flowing flocks of raven hair. Her hip's swayed seductively with each step until the panic that had been building in Alex's chest was washed away by a wave of desire. The only feature that remained from the painting was her eyes. They burned wickedly as she drew near. Her movements reminded him of a wild cat stalking and toying with its prey. Every move she made through the room was filled with liquid smoothness.

Finally she approached Alex and grabbed him by the shoulders. The feel of her hands on his skin filled him with a rush of euphoria. His head swam when she leaned forward and pressed her cold lips to his waiting mouth. The rest of the world faded away for just a moment as he held this beautiful woman in his arms.

Suddenly Alex became aware of the fact that he could not move. His entire body was as stiff as a board and there was a pressure on his lungs. He tried to break free from the feeling but his entire body melted into the touch of Head Mistress DelMonica. Without warning the scene changed. Alex found himself laying flat on his back in the Attic bedroom with the ghostly woman stretched on top of him. Her body writhed and pulsated as she pressed down on his chest with both hands. Her cold hands felt as though they were wrapped tightly around his lungs. Any time he tried to suck in breath the cold feeling would spread. He tried to shove her off, but his arms and legs refused to obey his commands. It was as though she had somehow petrified his entire body.

By now the euphoria had been replaced with utter terror. Alex found himself unable to draw a breath or even move. All the while the woman continued to writhe against him and press her icy lips to his skin. Every time she did Alex felt her hands tighten around his lungs. He tried to cry out for help but not even his voice would obey him. A numb sensation began to filter into Alex's arms and legs without warning.

Alex was finally able to pull himself from the dream enough to wake up. When he opened his eyes he almost screamed, but he was still paralyzed. There on top of him was the same woman from his dream. However, while he had dreamt of a sensual beauty the reality before him more closely resembled a rotting corpse. The dark hair that had been so lovely now clung to the scalp in scattered clumps. Cracked yellow flesh stretched sickeningly across the old bones. Alex tried to hold his breath but the stench of rotting meat filled his nose. If his body had not been paralyzed he was sure that he would have vomited.

When she noticed that her victim had woken up the creature that had once been Head Mistress DelMonica floated off of his body and into the air with a sickening grin. The door to the room opened and he watched as she floated down the stairs and into the darkened corridor. He didn't try to move until he saw the door to the room close tightly. When it did he automatically sat up in bed and hugged his knees. For a long time he tried to catch his breath, but every time he thought he had control he would suffer another coughing fit.

Finally the panic dulled and Alex could breathe again he was left with the feeling of utter violation. Something had happened to him while he was asleep and he was powerless to stop it. It came as no surprise when Alex realized that he was soaked in a cold sweat. He curled into a tight ball and sat trying to get himself warm.

Alex lost track of how long he sat like that. The only thing he remembered was the first rays of the sun peaking through the shutters of the attic window. When he saw the light he got out of the bed and went into the connected bathroom to take a shower.

Every muscle in his body ached as he moved, but the hot water helped to ease the stiffness somewhat. Sometime during his shower Alex had convinced himself that the dream had been a result of his fever. It was the only thing that made sense. He decided that the only way to make sure was to see the painting one last time before he left.

Once Alex was dried and dressed he stuffed everything in his bag and ran down the stairs. All he wanted now was to try and get back on the road. When he approached the painting of the headmistress Alex was struck by the curious change in the woman's face. At first he thought that his eyes were playing tricks on him, but when he looked closer the change was clear. When he first laid eyes on the painting, the head mistress looked as though she could be at least in her late thirties. But this morning her face looked more like it belonged to the woman from his dream. A chill ran up his spine as his dream was brought back to the front of his mind.

Alex turned away from the horrible picture and walked quickly downstairs towards the lobby. When he got there his eyes locked on a yellow sheet of paper taped to the front door. The writing on the paper made his heart sink.

"Dear Guests," the note read. "Due to weather conditions this area has been placed under a level three snow emergency. This means that anyone caught on the roads will be subject to prosecution. We understand many of you are trying to get home for the holidays, and because of this inconvenience all rooms will be half priced until the emergency is lifted. Thank you for your patience. The Fairfield Inn Staff."

Alex stared at the notice for what felt like an eternity. Another night in the attic room was out of the question. He had given up all pretext that his vision of the night before had been brought on by a fever. Something strange had happened to him the night before and he would be damned if he was just going to let it happen again. When he thought about waking up to the feeling of that hideous corpse writhing on top of him he started to feel violated. Something had done things to him and he had been powerless to stop it.

By the time breakfast came around Alex was still so shaken that he could barely handle the human interaction. Just looking at the faces around him brought back the first part of his dream, but it was better to be with people. He knew somehow that whatever had attacked him the night would not return while he was in the middle of a crowd. He sat alone at a table in the dining room pushing around a few scraps of egg and toast when he saw Carl approach him.

"You look like about ten miles of bad road." The older his man said his voice filled with concern. "Did you have a rough night?" Alex started to laugh at the older man's greeting, but the laugh was soon buried by a coughing fit that threatened to turn his stomach. Carl offered him a glass of ice water to help clear his throat.

"Sit down," Alex said and looked at the older man gratefully. Over the next several minutes Alex recounted the events of the night before. He finished by recounting the change in the Head Mistress's portrait. A grave expression stretched across Carl's face as he processed the information that he was given.

When Alex finished the older man took a moment to think before he tried to advise his younger friend.

"I want to see this painting." Carl said after a moment.

"All right," Alex said after a moment's hesitation. "Let's go then." The two men rose and made their way through the hallways to the painting. The face was the same as it had been when Alex last saw it. Carl studied the portrait closely. He was about to reach up and touch the surface of the portrait when Alex reached out and grabbed his wrist.

"I don't think that's a good Idea."

"Why not?" Carl asked with a note of surprise in his voice.

"I don't know. Just a feeling." Alex looked over his shoulder at the painting. His flesh began to crawl at the sight of the Head Mistress's mocking eyes. When he looked back at the older man his head began to swim. Just being close to the picture made him feel as though his fever were returning. A fresh coughing fit tore through his lungs. He looked pleadingly at Carl who seemed to be moved by the display.

The two men left the hallway and made their way to Carl's room. Unlike the Attic room it was furnished in an old fashioned but simple style. There were stacks of books and three ring binders on every flat surface of the room. Carl pointed to one of the two beds and Alex took that as his cue to sit down. His cough had subsided not long after they got away from the picture but he still felt so drained. The older man turned around and started sifting through a stack of papers until he evidently found what he was looking for. He offered the paper to Alex who took it without question.

"From what you told me it sounds like DelMonica has become some form of Boo Hag." He said pointing at the paper in Alex's hand. On it was a sketch of an old woman sitting naked across a man's chest as he lay in bed. Alex shuddered at the similarity between the picture and his experience of the night before.

"What's a Boo Hag?" He asked.

"It's a dark spirit that has to feed on the life-force of others. It picks someone and drains them of all of their energy while they sleep. They obtain the energy by 'riding' their victim" Carl crossed himself as he spoke. "The ideal way to deal with this would be to find a way to get you out of this place. If we don't then the Hag is going to come for you again, and I think if she does then you are done for."

This news made Alex's stomach turn. He already knew that there was no way to leave the Fairfield Inn for at least one more night. The winter storm had blocked the roads so badly that it would be at least another day before the plow trucks would be able to clear the mounds of snow that had developed overnight.

"I can't leave," He said in a defeated voice. "The snow around my car is so high that I can't even see it out there." Alex put his face in his hands and sighed. He could think of no way out of the situation. Carl put an encouraging hand on his young friends shoulder. When he did Alex felt a little swell of hope.

"If we can't get you out of here," Carl said in a determined whisper. "Then we're going to have to find a way to stop the Hag before she can feed on you again." Carl went back to searching through his papers as Alex looked on. After a few minutes he opened an old book and flipped through a few pages. As he watched Carl frantically search Alex's eyelids began to droop. He fought to stay awake, but eventually sleep overtook him. Alex spent the next few hours splayed out on top of Carl's bed in a deep and dreamless sleep while the older man dove headlong into a stack of books.

Alex woke to the sound of approaching footsteps. He opened his eyes and sat up in bed like a shot. When he did he saw Carl standing over him holding a tattered three ring binder.

"I think I found it." He said with a grin. He held out the binder for Alex to see. The page was covered with symbols. Alex looked at the page for a moment before pointing to the symbol that he had seen on the painting.

"That's the symbol that the head mistress wears around her neck."

"It's the symbol for eternity." Carl said. "The infinity loop that continues forever. She wore it around her neck at all times. At least that's what I gathered from my studies."

"What does it have to do with This Boo Hag thing?"

"According to the stories, DelMonica was trying to make herself immortal when she died."

"How did she die?" Alex asked without thinking.

"No one knows for sure. The school had been closed for years and no one came here much back then. DelMonica still went to town to do her shopping, but beyond that no one interacted with her. Eventually she stopped going into town at all. About a month after she had stopped going to town some of the locals came looking. They found her body in the Attic; she had apparently poisoned herself accidently. No one knows for sure exactly what she took, or when she had died. But it was obvious that she had been dead for quite some time." Alex shuddered at the memory of the rotting corpse that floated away from him towards the stairs. If Carl had noticed he gave no sign.

"When they searched through her effects the police found a document that detailed DelMonica's burial arrangements. It also stipulated that the painting of DelMonica should always be hung out of respect for her position in the house." When he finished Carl's face lit up like a light. He rose from where he had been sitting and reached out to Alex. "She left the room." He said in an excited voice.

"What?"

"She left the room. Last night, the ghost of the Head Mistress left the Attic. She's obviously tied to something in the house. At first I thought it was the room, but maybe it's something completely different." Carl sat quietly contemplating his own words for a moment. Suddenly, he shot up from his seat and looked Alex in the eye. "She left the room   "he said after a long pause.

"What?" the younger man asked in a confused voice.

"DelMonica, you said that last night when you woke up she floated away from you and down the main stairs. That means that her spirit isn't attached to the room. It has to be attached to something else entirely."

"Like the painting." Alex said after a moment. It was so simple that he hated himself for taking so long to figure out the answer. The more he thought about it the more sense it made. It explained the way that the painting had changed after Alex's dream.

"Exactly." Carl said with a grin.

"We have to destroy it." Alex shouted as he jumped to his feet. The sudden movements made his head swim and he had to sit back down.

"How would you propose we do that?" Carl asked. It was obvious that the older man had considered this plan of action and found some fault with it. "If the painting is really possessed then it won't be as simple as just taking a knife to the canvas. Something with real dark power has to be disposed of delicately."

"What do you mean?"

"I mean that in most cases you need to drive the spirit out before you destroy the possessed item. Otherwise you just have more pieces that you have to collect to purify." Alex sat and thought for a while before he spoke again.

"So how do we purify the painting?"

"I don't know, but I think I have an Idea." The two men sat together and planned their next move. They had to act together if they were going to be successful. By the time dinner came around both men knew exactly what they were going to do.

Dinner was a quiet event for Alex. Food was the last thing on his mind at the moment. In fact he only came down to dinner because Carl had reminded him that he needed his strength for the night to come. Alex was still feeling weak. The few hours of sleep he had gotten in Carl's room had refreshed him slightly, but his body still ached and he had to stop eating frequently in order to fight back coughing fits. As a result of his condition the other guests gave the pair a wide berth in the dining room. The two preferred it that way. They sat in the same corner seat and ate that they had the night before and ate in silence.

About half way through the meal Alex looked up and saw Mrs. Fairfield approaching him from across the room. The old woman rubbed her hands together nervously as she walked. Something was obviously on her mind. When she got to the table Carl greeted her with a warm smile. Alex in turn nodded to her respectfully but declined to give a proper greeting. After a moment Mrs. Fairfield leaned down to Alex and whispered in his ear.

"I was wondering if I could talk to you in private for a few minutes." She said in a voice that held more concern that Alex had expected. He rose from his seat stiffly and followed the old woman to the lobby just as she had the night before with her husband.

When they got to the lobby Mrs. Fairfield shut the door behind her and turned to look at the young man. Every move she made betrayed her concern for his well being. She wrung her hands more feverishly than she had before. It was obvious that she was unsure of how to begin the conversation. After a moment she cleared her throat and spoke.

"I was worried when I did not see you at lunch today. You looked so ill at breakfast that I was worried that you were coming down with something serious. But when I went upstairs to check on you I found your room empty."

"I spent the day with Carl," Alex said stiffly. "If it's alright with you I'd like to stay with him for the night. I'll gladly pay for part of his room costs for the night."

"That won't be necessary." The old woman replied with a relieved smile. "I hope that the room did not cause your illness," she added sheepishly.

"I think you know exactly what caused it." Alex snapped before he could stop himself. He instantly regretted saying it. The old woman flinched as though he had struck her in the face. Her expression softened any remaining resentment that Alex had held towards her. "I'm sorry," he said after a second. "I know you didn't plan for this to happen."

"I should have expected it." She said after a moment's silence. "I've known since we bought this place that there was something wrong with that room. That's why I forced my husband to convert it to storage space. I just hoped that maybe with the circumstances…" Her voice trailed off into a frustrated sigh. Alex put a hand on the old woman's shoulder and forced a smile. He knew what she was trying to say.

"So you believe that the room is haunted?"

"The whole Inn is haunted," she said flatly. Alex looked at her in shock. "When My husband and I bought the building I remember hearing voices in rooms that we hadn't even renovated yet. I tried to tell Andrew, but he just shrugged it off and told me that I was just being silly." Alex bristled at his own memories of the old man's callous attitude. The old woman seemed not to notice as she continued. "I can still see things, usually just out of the corner of my eye. I've even seen that painting upstairs change. One day the woman will be old and gray, but the next she looks like a young girl in her twenties."

"Yeah, she's like that now." Alex nodded as he spoke. A cold feeling gripped the base of his spine as he thought about the events of the last twenty four hours.

"Can I give you some advice?" The old woman suddenly asked.

"Of course." He said with a smile.

"Don't go into the attic tonight. Stay in the room with Carl and don't even try to sleep up there. I would hate for anything bad to happen to you again."

"I promise I won't go up there again." Alex said politely. Deep down he knew that he was lying straight to the old woman's face, but there was no way around it. He made his excuse and returned to the dining room.

Just as he had the night before Alex sat in the dining room until all of the other guests had gone to bed. He watched the fire dwindle down to a few dying embers and listened to the ticking of the clock in the hall. When the clock struck nine he pushed himself to his feet and started towards the stairs. He was happy that the path to Carl's room did not lead him past the painting of the head mistress. His nerve was shaky enough without having to look at that horrible face again.

Alex tried the door to Carl's room and found it unlocked just as the older man had promised. He walked into the room and looked around. The stacks of papers and books sat just as they had when the two men left for dinner. Carl was nowhere to be seen in the room. He must be out taking care of his part of the plan. Alex changed into a pair of sweatpants and a t shirt before lying in the bed that he had fallen asleep on earlier in the day. Although he was still exhausted he found it difficult to fall asleep at first. His mind was just too active to allow him to doze sufficiently. He remembered how quickly he had fallen asleep the night before. Could it be that the Boo Hag had some sort of hypnotizing effect?

As if in answer to his question Alex's eyes suddenly became heavy. He fought to stay awake for as long as he could, but his eyelids continued to get heavier. Just as Alex was about to fall asleep he saw a shadow move off in the corner of his eye. He looked over and saw a silhouetted figure approaching him. As the figure drew nearer Alex tried to push himself up into a defensive position only to find that his limbs would not obey his commands. A bolt of fear shot through him when he realized that he was paralyzed again.

When the figure finally came into view Alex recognized the face of the Head Mistress. Her face was lit up by a triumphant grin. Alex tried to call out for help but the paralysis had extended to his vocal cords. Head Mistress DelMonica leaned forward and looked him in the eyes. There was no emotion in the dead glassy stare, but in the back of his mind Alex could hear a malicious chuckle. The woman's mouth didn't move, but Alex was sure he could hear the voice of a woman. The soft voice raked at his ears like nails at a chalk board.

"Foolish young man," the voice said bitterly. "Did you think that I would not know where you were tonight?" A peal of disembodied laughter filled Alex's head and made him wince with pain. The sound stabbed at his senses like jagged glass. "I could sense your life force from a mile away. Once I have tasted such sweet milk, I would go to the ends of the earth to find it again."

The shadow's around the head mistress fluttered and revealed her creamy white skin as she threw a leg over Alex's body. She pressed her hands tightly against his chest and leaned forward until her lips were nearly touching his own. As she did this the glamour of her beauty faded away and Alex could see the true being beneath the facade. Once again he found himself face to face with a rotting corpse. Alex's fear transferred into anger and revulsion at the sight of the decayed flesh of the creature before him. Still, he forced himself to look until he locked his eyes on the silver charm around the hag's neck. If he could just move his hands he could take that charm, and then he would tear this creature limb from limb.

A feeling of heaviness began to overtake Alex's body as the Hag began to feed. He lay frozen on his back and tried to block the Hag from draining his life but there was nothing that he could do. Frozen as he was he had to trust that Carl would stick to his part of the plan?

As if in answer to Alex's unspoken prayers the hag pushed away from him and cocked her head to one side. The sickening smile faded from her lips and she looked down at Alex with a look of utter shock.

"My Portrait!" The voice screamed in his head. The hag was about to rise when smoke began to pour from her body. The hag let out a long piercing shriek to the sky and started to back away. Alex felt the feeling return to his arms and legs. It was as though someone had flipped a switch and his body would once again respond to his will. He shot out an arm and punched the hag full in the face. She rocked to one side and tried to regain her balance atop him. For a moment Alex felt his muscles tightening but he threw another desperate punch to the face of the hag and the feeling vanished. His fist sunk deep into the decayed flesh and he felt the jawbone crack behind the pressure of the blow.

The third time Alex reached out towards the creature he closed his fist around the small silver infinity symbol around her neck. With a strong jerk he snapped the chain that held the charm in place. Head Mistress DelMonica let out another shriek that shook the Inn to its very foundations. When it ended the air reverberated with the echoes of the cry. Alex pushed the rotting corpse to the ground and leapt out of the bed. By now the smoke was flowing from every pore of the creature that lay before him. Alex held out the infinity charm in front of him and showed it to the Head Mistress. When she was about to reach out to touch it Alex stomped on her arm and pressed down until he could feel the bones snap.

Carl came into the room a moment later still holding the remains of the burning painting in his hand. He looked at the creature on the floor and Alex could tell that the older man was shocked.

"Hold her down." Alex said to the older man. In his turn Carl stepped on the chest of the hag and pressed down as hard as he could. Alex removed his foot from the thing's body and strode across the room to one of the tables. When he got there he threw the silver charm onto a metal plate that he had found in the kitchen and picked up a hammer. He raised the hammer over his head and drove it down onto the symbol of the Hag's power with as much force as he could muster.

The charm warped slightly after the first impact and Alex had to raise the hammer and try again to break one of the loops that made up the symbol. When the charm broke the hag let out one final wail before it crumbled to ash on the floor of the room. Alex looked down at the spot where the charm he had taken from the creature had been and saw a small pile of dust.

Outside the room Alex could hear the sound of rushing footsteps. He looked at Carl who put a finger to his lips and shook his head. There was a knock at the door and both men went to answer it.

On the other side of the door stood Mr. and Mrs. Fairfield and several of the Inn's guests. Most of them wore looks that spoke volumes of their confusion. Alex smiled to himself when he saw that Mrs. Fairfield alone seemed to have a clue what was going on.

"What the Hell just happened?" Mr. Fairfield spat at the pair of men on the other side of the door. Carl and Alex just exchanged a look.

"I was just about to ask you the same thing." Alex said after a moment. "I was just sleeping when I heard somebody scream loud enough to wake the dead."

"The sound came from this room." Mr. Fairfield said with a stern look. "I know it did." Alex smiled politely at the old man and stepped back from the door. The crowd slowly filtered in through the doorway and looked around the room. The confusion on their faces increased when they saw nothing out of the ordinary. Alex looked around the room with them. He even opened the closet doors so that everyone could see that they were empty.

"I don't see anything that would make a scream like that do you?" he asked after a few minutes. The crowd all shook their heads and Mr. Fairfield stormed out of the room with a sour expression. Mrs. Fairfield stayed behind and looked at the two men. After a long moment she reached into the pocket of her bath robe and produced the final scrap of the painting.

"I saw this under the bed and snagged it before my husband could look." She said offering the scrap to Alex. "You would do best to destroy it quickly."

"How did you know?" he asked.

"I told you I've had dreams ever since I moved in to this house." She said with a wink and rejoined the group.

Carl fell into one of the overstuffed chairs in the room and sighed heavily. Alex looked over his shoulder at the older man and smiled.

"I was starting to worry that you couldn't get the lighter to light." He said quietly.

"I had to carry that heavy picture down to the fireplace to get it to burn." Carl replied after a moment. "The lighter just didn't have enough juice on its own." He laid his head back in the chair and lay silent for a moment. Alex thought he had fallen asleep when he suddenly spoke again. "It was weird."

"What was?"

"The painting. Head Mistress DelMonica was in the painting one minute, the next she just faded out of view. So I scooped it up and ran down the stairs as fast as I could. I had a feeling that time was of the essence."

"You can say that again." Alex said as he lay back down on the bed. Neither man said another word that night. Instead they both faded off to sleep.

The next morning the snow had melted enough for Alex and the other stranded travelers to get back on the road, but before he did Alex had to make one quick stop. He walked into the dining room quietly and walked over to the fireplace. Then he pulled the final piece of the portrait from his pocket and tossed it into the fire. As he watched it burn Alex felt some of his energy return. Then he packed up the last of his belongings and jumped into his car. As he drove away Alex told himself that he might like to return to the Fairfield Inn someday.

A few years later Alex was hunting through the shelves at his local book store when he saw a familiar face on the new authors' shelf. He picked up the book and thumbed through the

pages. When he found the entry on the Fairfield Inn, his heart sank.

The story said that only a few months after his first visit to the inn

there was a fire that originated in the Attic. Mr. and Mrs. Fairfield

were killed in the inferno and the Fairfield Inn burned to the

ground.

Christmas Waltz

The moon is full outside my bedroom window, and I can hear the orchestra warming up downstairs. My husband's party is beginning; soon I must make my entrance. I take one final look in the mirror; my white dress practically glows in the lamplight. This will be a night to remember.

Madame Gwendolyn lit the candles on the table one by one. Each point of light brought the room into more clarity. As she lit the final candle the old woman looked around the room at the circle of people gathered. There wasn't an empty seat at the table. She allowed herself a small smile as she sat back in her chair and nodded. If everything went according to plan, this would be a night to remember.

I make my way through the upstairs hallway towards the Main hall where the party is taking place. On my way I exchange pleasantries with Mr. Daniels. The silly man has gotten himself turned around on his way to the cloak room. I point him in the right direction before I take my place at the head of the grand staircase. I peak around the corner of the balcony and see that the servants have done a marvelous job of decorating the hall for our party. There is an enormous tree in the center of the room decorated with beautiful ribbons and candles. I can hear the bustle of my husband's guests in the Main hall. They are waiting for me to make my grand entrance so that our party can begin. I catch the eye of Figgins the Butler and make the sign for him to announce me. The old man clears his throat and begins to speak.

"Ladies and Gentlemen…"

"We are here tonight to try and contact the spirit of Sarah Blackthorn, also known as the Bloody Woman." Madame

Christmas Spirits Rueckert

Gwendolyn Sais in her tired whisper. The members of the circle lean closer to hear the old woman more clearly. "She only appears on Christmas Eve because that was the night of her annual party. It was at this party that John Blackthorn stabbed his wife to death in view of all of the guests. There are those who believe that she is responsible for the death of the young man last Christmas Eve." Madame Gwendolyn looked around the room once more. Her piercing eyes locked on the small Christmas tree in the center of the table. With any luck this focus object would be just what she needed to bring back the spirit. "Now, everyone join hands and we will begin." The old woman holds out her hands waits to feel the warmth of human touch. When each member of the circle locks hands she closes her eyes and begins to focus.

The orchestra plays my favorite Christmas song as I glide down the stairs into the main hall. The eyes of the whole room are locked on me. When I reach the bottom of the stairs I hold out my hands to my husband who is waiting for me. He bows and kisses them gently before he leads me out to the dance floor. The orchestra changes their tempo and the dance begins. I whirl around the room entranced by the beautiful music. I never want the song to end...

The séance began with a moment of silence so that Madame Gwendolyn could focus her ability so that she could find a gateway into the land of death. The old woman locked her eyes on the dancing flame of the candles and let herself be mesmerized by the gentle movements of the fire. Suddenly the old woman cocks her head to one side. Off in the distance she hears the sound of a small orchestra playing old Christmas songs. The music started to increase in volume. Eventually everyone at the circle could hear it playing and Madame Gwendolyn could feel the tension in the room.

I can feel my husband's arm wrapped tightly about the waist while we spin across the dance floor. My feet feel as though they are floating on air. The festive music spreads throughout the room brightening the atmosphere. I can feel the smile spreading across my face as we move. We haven't danced like this since my husband returned from the war. I feel my cheeks flush when he leans down to kiss me.

Christmas Spirits Rueckert

"Sarah Blackthorn," Madame Gwendolyn called out in a deep clear voice that echoed throughout the room. "We call upon you to show yourself this evening. Come to the sound of my voice Sarah Blackthorn." The echo of the old woman's voice filled the room. As the echoes died Madame Gwendolyn felt the temperature of the room drop several degrees. A cold breeze blew down the back of her neck from the direction of the grand staircase. The muscles in her back tightened in response to this feeling. "Someone is approaching." She announced to the awe struck audience.

When the song ends a hush falls over our guests. I look to my husband and see sheer terror in his eyes. I follow his gaze to the head of the grand staircase where I see a tall man in a black opera cloak watching us. Figgins approaches the gentleman to ask for his invitation and I watch the two engage in a short conversation. The gentleman in the black cloak waves a hand to Figgins and the old butler turned to address the gathered crowd.

The cold wind circled the table and blew out all but one of the candles. Madame Gwendolyn squeezed the hands of the person on either side of her to encourage them to hold the circle tight.

Behind her she could hear the sound of footsteps descending the

staircase. The other members of the circle turned to see who was

coming, but all they could make out was a faint red mist. As it

descended the stairs the disembodied music stopped.

"Ladies and Gentlemen, It is my duty to introduce Mister

Abaddon." The gentleman in the black cloak bowed formally

before shrugging out of his cloak and tosses it into Figgins' arms.

The name struck me as familiar but I could not place it. I look at

the gentleman for a moment trying to recall where my husband and

I may have met him before. Mr. Abaddon looks at me and smiles.

My husband tenses when he notices that the gentleman is walking

towards us. I have to hold him tightly to keep him from turning to

walk away.

"Sarah Blackthorn," The old woman said to the mist as it

floated across the room. "Give us a sign that you are with us." The

mist halted its procession through the room and flew quickly to the

old woman's side. It swirled around and through her until the two

had become one. Madame Gwendolyn's head slumped forward

onto her chest for a moment. When she lifted it again there had been some untold metamorphosis. The old woman looked around the room and opened her mouth to speak.

Mr. Abaddon approaches us with a smile that makes my skin crawl to look at. I still do not recognize the gentleman, but I intend to extricate myself from the acquaintance very soon. As he draws closer my husband steps forward as though to guard me from the man with the unsettling eyes. For a moment I find it strange, this is the first time since he returned from the war my husband seems to be afraid. It is clear that Mr. Abaddon senses this because his smile grows broader. I can see from this distance that his canine teeth were long and sharply pointed. He offers his hand to my husband but draws it back after a moment. When he speaks his voice reminds me of the sound that precedes a winter storm.

"Tell us Sarah, do you remember the night of your death?" The old woman said in a loud commanding voice. There was a single knock on the Table. The entire circle buzzed with excitement at what seemed to be a direct response. Madame Gwendolyn smiled to herself. After more than one hundred years it

was time to discover the truth about the Bloody Woman of Blackthorn house.

"Good evening Mr. Blackthorn. I trust you have not forgotten me."

"Of course not." My husband says with a shaky voice. After a moment his shoulders slump slightly. The effect of Mr. Abaddon's presence is felt by more than just my husband and I. A shudder spreads throughout the room and I see several people hide their eyes from the tall man in black.

Mr. Abaddon looks around the room and back to my husband. "It appears that I have arrived at an inopportune time. Is there somewhere that we can speak privately while your guests return to their festivities?" The tone of his voice sent a chill up my spine. I have to close my eyes and suppress another shudder.

"We could go to my study." My husband offers reluctantly after several moments. Mr. Abaddon reaches out and takes him around the shoulder to lead him through the crowd. Before they leave he looks back at me with his unnerving smile.

"Not to worry Mrs. Blackthorn. I won't be keeping your husband long. We just have some Business to take care of." The way he says the word business turns my stomach. I can think of nothing that my husband would have to do with this man. I can only nod my assent and the two men soon disappear into the crowd.

Across the room from the séance table a door opened and closed loudly. Everyone at the table jumped accept for Madame Gwendolyn.

"Is that the room where you were killed Sarah?" The door swung open and slammed shut a second time in answer to this question. For several minutes Madame Gwendolyn asked dozens of questions about the night that Sarah Blackthorn was murdered. Each time there would be a single knock. The gathered audience sat amazed by what they were witnessing. Eventually the responses to the questions became faster, sometimes Madame Gwendolyn would only have half of her question asked when the knock came. Everyone was so caught up in the responses that no one noticed the cluster of dark mist forming at the top of the grand stair case.

I follow my husband and Mr. Abaddon with my eyes until they vanish through the door that leads into the study. With the strange man in black out of sight everyone in the room breathe a sigh of relief. It isn't long before the orchestra starts to play a quick tempoed song to liven the room. I make my rounds as the hostess and thank everyone for coming. We make small talk about the weather and the services that will take place tomorrow. All the while my eyes keep straying back to the door that my husband went through. The minutes since the two men went to the study feel like hours. An uneasiness starts to creep into my mind. What are they doing in that room? I must find out.

Suddenly the entity in the room stopped answering Madame Gwendolyn's questions. Instead it began to knock randomly on every hard surface in the room. The people in the circle began to feel uneasy about the knocking.

"She's trying to tell us something." One member said breathlessly.

"It's just rats in the walls." Another added.

"Someone else is coming." Madame Gwendolyn said after a moment. Her words caught the attention of the entire room. Even The spirit stopped its erratic tapping. "Someone dark. Is it your Husband Sarah? Is that why you are frightened?" After a moment there were two distinct knocks on the table in front of the old woman.

As I work my way through the gathered crowd the uneasiness grows. The guests all seem to be avoiding the door to the study. It is apparent that they do not want to involve themselves with whatever business is being transacted. I hold my breath and listen for a moment at the door. My husband's hushed voice floats through the door. I cannot make out what he is saying, but the words are filled with a passion that I have never known him to possess. The response from Mr. Abaddon comes out in one long hiss that chills my blood. Finally I cannot bear the tension any more. My hand turns the door knob of its own accord. When I step into the study I am hit with a sensation of utter panic.

Madame Gwendolyn sat dumbfounded for a moment. If the other entity in the room wasn't John Blackthorn then who could it be? The old woman cleared her throat and began to speak again.

"Sarah Blackthorn. Is the spirit approaching that of the one who

killed you?"

One knock echoed through the room.

"But your husband is not responsible for your death?" The

old woman asked. Two distinct taps sounded on the floor beside

the séance table.

My husband and Mr. Abaddon are standing on opposite

sides of the large oak desk. Each man is leaning forward so closely

to the other's face that they are practically nose to nose. I gasp

when I notice a small trickle of blood running from my husband's

ear. His face is a mask of anger and hatred that I have never seen in

my life. I believe that if he were capable at this moment he would

throttle Mr. Abaddon to death with his bare hands. Neither man

realizes that I have entered the room. Instead they are arguing

passionately about something that is yet unclear to me.

"I am now addressing the dark presence in this place. I ask

you to make yourself known to us just as Sarah did." There was no response. Madame Gwendolyn strained to hear even the slightest of taps but there was no sound coming from the house. Whatever this entity was, it was not interested in playing games. The old woman tried one more time but with the same effect. She shifted restlessly in her seat for a moment before calling out to Sarah one more time. This time even the specter of the Bloody woman was unable to answer.

"Do you deny the service that I rendered you?" Mr. Abaddon hisses into my husband's face. The sickening smile has given way to an expression of utter contempt. For the first time my attention is drawn to the stranger's eyes. They appear an unnatural shade of green in the hazy lamplight. They gazes remain locked for a long moment, and then my husband hangs his head.

"No, I cannot deny it." His voice comes out like that of a whipped dog. Mr. Abaddon straightens his back and an expression of Triumph fills his glowing eyes.

"I spared your life on that battle field, and what was the price that I demanded from you for that mercy?"

"You said you would come back in three years." Whispers my husband. "The price for that time was my soul."

"And I have come to collect that Debt Jonathan Blackthorn. Tonight you will come with me, one way or another." I suddenly remember where I have heard the name Abaddon before. He is of the chief demons of hell. If my loving husband made a deal with this creature then all is lost.

The air in the room became thick with moisture. Madame Gwendolyn started to speak but her voice was drowned by a cough. For a long moment she struggled against the feeling that the dark spirit were trying to take control of her body. Suddenly there was a change in the old woman. She cocked her head to one side and began to speak in a voice that sounded like it was emanating from the throat of a vicious beast.

I go to comfort my husband. His muscles tense when I lay a hand protectively on his shoulder and I can see his eyes fill with tears. I wrap him tightly in my arms and look to the creature in human form that stands before us.

"You will not take my husband. Not tonight and not ever."
I say with as much authority as I can. The demon leans closer to
me and I can smell brimstone and sulfur in the air. It is clear to me
that his eyes do not need the lamplight to glow. They are imbued
with an unnatural luminescence of their own.

"How do you intend to stop me?" He growls. All humor
and emotion drains from the voice and it now sounds like the
growl of a great beast waiting to pounce.

*"I am Abaddon the destroyer. I took the life of that woman,
and I snuffed out the soul of the child that was growing in her."
The old woman growled in a voice that was not her own. The other
members of the circle backed away from Madame Gwendolyn and
released their hands to break the circle. The creature inside the old
woman laughed. It sounded like the rolling of thunder across a
windy sky.*

*"The old witch resists me." Said the voice of the demon. "I
cannot hold to her mortal frame, but know that this is not the end. I
shall return." Madame Gwendolyn began to cough as the black*

mist flowed from her mouth and nose and collected into a cloud

several feet over the table. When it had exited the old woman's

body the dark spirit circled the room and made its way back up the

grand staircase when it left.

Despite the fear welling up within my heart I stand straight and look the demon in the face. I try to think of a way to drive the evil thing from our home. Suddenly I notice my husband's silver letter opener sitting on the desk. Just as I am about to move my hand to grasp it the demon flips the heavy wood over into the nearest wall. Then he reaches out his hand and I feel myself lifting into the sky. His green eyes glow with a cold fury that can only be seen in the darkest of nightmares. I struggle to move, but my body is frozen in the air. My husband has dropped to his knees to beg the demon to let me go. But I can see in those firry eyes that his petitions hold no sway.

Madame Gwendolyn slumped forward in her chair for what

felt like an eternity. The members of the circle started intently

waiting for the old woman to take a breath. When she finally

inhaled there was a collective sigh of relief. Her ordeal had visibly taken a lot out of the old woman. Finally she rose to her feet and looked around the room. The temperature had risen several degrees and off in the distance she was sure that she could hear the town clock strike midnight. The night of the Bloody Woman was over. Even though no one would believe the truth about the events of that night.

"I had planned to take your soul John Blackthorn, but now I see a better prize before me. I will rob you of that which you have so long hoped. There is more spirit in her than you let on, but I think she will do nicely. Tonight I will take your loving wife, as well as the child inside of her." The demons lips open to reveal a row of pointed teeth. He approaches me with the silver letter opener in one hand. I feel the pain as over and over again the demon pierces my skin with the point of the letter opener. Finally my body falls to the floor. My beautiful white dress has been stained red by my blood. The creature has gone, and in its place only my husband and I remain. I lay there still for a moment and listen to my husband scream my name until his voice fades into a distant memory.

Madame Gwendolyn looked around the table at the scared faces of her audience. She sat silently for a moment longer before she nodded.

"Sarah Blackthorn was not killed by her husband." The old lady said confidently. "Her death came at the hands of the same dark spirit that tried to harm us here tonight. I believe that this same dark spirit is responsible for the death of that young man last Christmas. Sadly we can prove nothing. All we can do is spread the truth as we experienced it here tonight." With that said Madame Gwendolyn rose from her seat and bowed her head to blow out the final candle which left the room in darkness. The only remaining illumination in the room came from a large window. Through it the moon shined bright and full in the winter sky.

The moon is full outside my bedroom window, and I can hear the orchestra warming up downstairs. My husband's party is beginning; soon I must make my entrance. I take one final look in the mirror; my red dress practically glows in the lamplight. This will be a night to remember.

The Gift

I hadn't planned on going into the antique shop that day, but the moment I saw the doll in the window I knew that I had to buy it. It was the perfect gift for Nicole. My wife used to collect porcelain dolls when she was a little girl. She barely spoke to me for a week when I accidently broke her favorite doll named Lucy three years ago. We had just gotten married and I was moving some things from her parents house into our apartment when I tripped on the steps. I tried to keep from falling on the box but somehow Lucy had slipped out and her delicate head shattered to a million pieces on the floor.

Lucy had been a gift from Nicole's late grandmother. She had comissioned the doll so that it would look just like Nicole. It was as close a likeness as you could get from a porcelain doll. When Lucy broke, I tried to find a doll to replace her but there was nothing out there that I could find. I thought about custom ordering a doll, but it was far more than I could afford. Eventually Nicole convinced me to give up the search. But when I saw the doll in the window my heart leapt. It was almost an exact copy of Lucy. The hair was slighlty darker, and the face had a few small differences but it was almost scary how much the two dolls resembled each other.

The inside of the store smelled strongly of mothballs, shelves lined with knickknacks and photos lined the walls. The center of the store was filled with an assortment of chairs and other furniture, an open path lead to a small counter with a cash register. the shop keeper looked like he should have been one of the items for sale. What little hair the poor old man had left was snow white and he could barely walk up to greet me when I entered. The old man pointed out several items; among them a beautifully carved desk that took up an entire corner of the dimly lit store. I tried to make it look like I was just browsing but my eyes kept straying back to the doll in the window. When the old man saw me looking, his eyes sparkled behind his glasses.

"You seem to have taken a fancy to Alison there young man." He said. "Poor girl has been sitting in that window for years just waiting for the right person to come along."

"It's perfect."

"You don't know much about dolls do you my young friend?" The old man said in a stern tone. "You never call one of these dolls an IT. Her name is Alison, at least that's what the person who sold her to me called her and it seems to suit her too." Here, let me get her down so you can take a closer look." The old man gently lifted the doll from its place in the window and offered it to me. I took the doll and looked at it clo. The craftsmanship of the doll was amazing. Her eyes looked as though they belonged to a real woman rather than a little porcelain doll.

"Nicole would love her." I said absently as I searched the doll for a price tag.

"Buying her for a young lady then?" The old man's smile broadened.

"My wife used to have a doll almost Identical to this one. She was devastated when it broke. I tried to find another one, but this is the first time I saw anything even close." I told him. "How much are you asking?"

"The pricetag is tied around her wrist." I looked at the little paper tag and my heart sank. Six hundred dollars was more than I could afford to pay, even for my wife's perfect christmas present. I offered the doll back to the old man who just shook his head. "I couldn't take her back." He said seriously.

"I'm sorry sir, I just can't afford to take her." I offered him the doll again but he persisted.

"Maybe we could come to some kind of deal? She had been sitting in that window for years. You are the first person to come in and even look at her twice. It seems like she has chosen you to take her home."

"Yes but sir." Before I could continue the old man held his hands up once more. My face began to burn as I let out a sigh of aggravation.

"I'll tell you what. Since Alison has taken such a liking to you. I'll give you a discount." I thought it was strange that the old man kept reffering to the doll as though it were a living breathing human being, but I decided it was probably just the old man's way of keeping his sanity with all of the time he spent in the store alone. I must admit the prospect of a discount did pique my interest.

"Then how much are you asking?" I asked, half expecting the price to still be far more than I could afford.

"One hundred fifty dollars." Before I could protest any more the old man looked me in the eye and smiled. "Call it a Christmas present from an old man." I wrote the old man a check and he put the doll in a box and gift wrapped it for me. On my way home I stopped and bought a card to go along with it.

My wife was still at work when I got home so I hid the doll as best I could and made dinner. We ate when Nicole got home and spent the rest of the evening watching television. before we went to bed Nicole found the box containing the doll and looked at me curiously.

"What's this?" She asked with a smile on her face. Her eye's lit up when I told her that I had found her Christmas present while I was out and about. She tried to convince me to let her open it but I held firm. Christmas was still four days away and I wanted it to be special. Nicole pouted a little but eventually she gave up and we went to bed.

I woke up in the middle of the night and to the sound of a child crying. It sounded like it was coming from every direction at once but I couldn't find a source for it. Nicole was sleeping soundlessly and didn't seem to hear a thing. I turned on my bedside lamp and looked around for any source of the sound. There was nothing in the room that could have made that sound. The television was off and there was no radio. My first thought was that one of the neighbors had been crying, but no one on our floor had kids. Not to mention the fact that the sound was coming from inside our bedroom. When I looked at the clock it was two thirty in the morning. The crying continued for a while then as suddenly as it started the room fell silent.

I double checked my phone and the television to make sure that neither of them had been responsible for the sound. The television had obviously been turned off for several hours, and my phone was set to silent so that it wouldn't go off if I got a late night e-mail. I even checked the rest of the apartment for disturbances, but nothing was out of place. The lack of anything that could have made the crying sound convinced me that I had drempt the whole thing. By the time I had gotten back to bed I didn't care about anything more than going back to sleep.

The next day Nicole told me about a strange dream that she had during the night. In her dream she was in her parents house and she saw Lucy in her old bedroom. But when she went to pick the doll up a little girl walked into the room and snatched it away. Before she could protest the girl shattered the doll on the floor. She said she had never seen the little girl before but there was something wrong with her. "Something about her just scared me." She added.

I tried not to show any emotion but I was a little rattled that Nicole was having dreams about Her doll when the one I had bought was sitting in a box in the next room. It never occurred to me that she would know about Alison. If she had peeked then she would have found another way to bring it up in discussion.

"Do you think it means anything?" I asked as innocently as I could. A voice in the back of my head told me to be careful how I broached the topic. If my wife was dreaming about dolls then it wouldn't do to make her suspicious. The last thing I wanted was to ruin the surprise after I had spent three years searching for the right doll.

"I don't know but that little girl scared me a little. I know it was just a dream, but I got the feeling that if I had tried to take Lucy back she would have hurt me somehow." Nicole shuddered as she said this and deilberately changed the topic. "Oh, I almost forgot. I will be getting home early today because we have to go to your cousin's calling hours."

"Poor old Larry," I said looking down at my cup of coffee. "Mom says she talked to him yesterday and he sounded like he had been drinking. But that doesn't sound like him. Larry was never much of a drinker."

"Can you blame him?" Nicole asked. "I mean, Janet had been missing for three days before they found her. To go from not knowing where the love of your life is to this. I'm surprised he is holding himself together at all." I reached out and touched Nicole's hand. She squeezed mine back gently before she got up and left for work.

Work was slow and tedious. I spent most of it sending the same report to four different departments. After that I had to make changes to the report my supervisor had sent me because the data was entered incorrectly. During my lunch break, I tried to get ahead on the work that I wouldn't be doing during the holidays so that I could finish up quickly and get to the funeral home on time.

When four o clock rolled around I was out the door and down the hall before my supervisor had time to ask me where I was going. I didn't want to explain to her that my cousin's wife had died in a car accident. Mostly because I had told her the day before and she had obviously already forgotten.

There were more people than I had expected to see at the calling hours. Janet was the kind of person who could make friends without even trying. It was sad to see her go, but my heart truly went out to her husband. Larry looked like he hadn't been sleeping well. I wanted to pull him aside and tell him that everything was going to be alright, but the line behind me was too long. Instead I gave him my condolences and promised to catch up with him soon.

The next two days passed quickly. By the time Christmas morning came along I had forgotten about everything accept for giving Nicole the doll. I almost gave it to her on Christmas eve but I held firm. I knew that she would love it as soon as she laid eyes on it. On her part Nicole wasn't making it easy to keep the secret. She kept trying to ask me questions that would give her clues as to the contents of the mysterious box.

Christmas Spirits Rueckert

We woke up early Christmas morning and went into the main room of the appartment. There were two wrapped boxes under the tree. I smiled when I saw the way that Nicole kept looking at the box that contained Alison. The excitement on her face made her look like a little girl.

"You should go first," I said offering her the box.

"No, You go first. I want to see you open yours."

"How about we go at the same time?" I suggested, to be honest we already knew we were going to do it this way. It had worked this way every year.

I handed Nicole the box that contained Alison and she slid the other box close enough for me to pick it up. It was a decent sized box covered in cartoon snowmen. I found the crease in the paper and pulled it appart in a long strip. Under the paper was a department store box and I almost groaned. Over the past few years I had become accustomed to holiday gifts being Nicole's opportunity to attempt to improve myz wardrobe.

I looked at my wife and noticed that she was still gently pulling on the bow that held the top on the box. I smiled at the difference between our unwrapping styles. I had no problem shreading the paper and tossing the box but Nicole treated every gift like a timebomb. She would unwrap it so carefully that the paper would still be useable for another gift.

I went back to the box in my lap and pulled back the lid. I was shocked to see a wrapped bundle packed tightly in the tissue paper. I tore through the wrapping of the bundle and smiled when I saw an antique copy of the complete works of Edgar Allan Poe.

My smile widened when I heard Nicole gasp. I looked up and saw her pull the doll out of the box and look at me with surprise.

"She looks just like Lucy!" She said breathlessly. "Where did you find her?" I told Nicole about the day at the antique shop. She laughed at me when I told her how the old man corrected me when I referred to the doll as an it. "Of course he did. You never refer to a doll like this as an it." Then she looked at the doll and nodded politely. "Hello Alison, I am very glad to meet you."

Nicole hugged the doll gently and adjusted her dress. When she did I noticed something metalic catching the light around the doll's neck. When I told her about it she looked at the front of the Alison's dress and found a small golden locket on a chain. She opened the locket and her face went pale.

"What's wrong?"

"Look at the picture." She gently took the locket off of Alison's neck and offered it to me. I looked closely and a chill ran down my spine. The picture in the locket was of a little girl with blond hair and sunken cheeks. She wore a grave expression and her eyes were dull and listless.

"That's one scary little girl."

"It's the girl from my dream." Nicole said with a note of panic creeping into her voice.

I spent the next half hour trying to convince Nicole that the girl in the locket had nothing to do with her dream. When she eventually calmed down I took the picture and threw it away. I kept the locket and told my wife that I would put a picture of her in it and put it back around the doll's neck later but she told me not to.

"When a doll like this has a photo it usually means it was made especially for that person. Just like Lucy was for me. Sometimes they would even use the child's own hair to make the doll more lifelike. That's what my grandmother did." Nicole was smoothing the doll's hair as she spoke. I was glad that she was happy with Alison. She took the doll into the bedroom and put her on the top of the bookcase with a her rag doll Buttons. When she came out she seemed to have forgotten all about the girl in the photo.

We ate breakfast together and spent the rest of the morning getting ready to go visit relatives. Our plan was to spend lunch with Nicole's parents and then drive up north to spend the evening with mine. While my wife was getting her coat, I loaded the rest of the gifts into the car and started the engine so that the heater would have a chance to warm the car.

Nicole and I enjoyed the rest of the day. I had to tell Nicole's parents the story about finding the doll in the antique shop. Her father smiled when he heard me mention the old man saying that Alison had "Chosen me" as he put it.

"Better hope the doll isn't the jealous type." He said with a smile. I winked at Nicole and she burst out laughing.

"I'm not too worried about that. I just hope I don't break this one."

"Oh don't worry about that, you aren't touching Alison Mr. Butterfingers. One broken doll is quite enough." Nicole nudged me with her elbow and it was my turn to laugh.

Dinner with my parents was the same. Gifts were exchanged and we spent the rest of the evening talking about recent events. My mother asked me if I had spoken to Larry since the funeral. I told her that he was spending time with his in laws but he promised he would come over for New Years.

On the way home Nicole told me that there was one more surprise waiting for me at home. She wouldn't tell me any more and I spent the rest of the drive trying to figure out what she could be hiding from me. My thought process was interrupted when I saw a the lights of the police car in front of our building. I pulled the car along the side of the squad car and asked the officer what was going on. He told me that one of the neighbors had called about a possible break in at our apartment. I quickly parked the car and the officer followed us up the stairs. When we got to the third floor the door to the aprtment was still locked. I handed the officer the key and he went into the apartment to look around before giving us the all clear.

"If someone did break in they already left. There is a little damage but I don't know if anything was taken. I'm sorry for the inconvenience, please let us know if there is anything missng. He gave me his card and tried to look reassuring. "Hopefully this hasn't ruined your holiday." He left us to enter our apartment alone.

Most of the house appeared to be untouched, there were a few things out of place but that was it.

The worst of the damage was in the bedroom. The room had been ransacked. Clothes and jewelry were thrown around the room. It looked like whoever had broken in was searching for something. Nicole and I spent the next hour cleaning up the mess. Luckily it looked like the intruder hadn't found what they were looking for. As far as we could tell nothing was missing. They hadnt even taken the money that was sitting on my bedside table.

The one thing in the room that looked like it had not been touched was Alison. The rag doll on the bookcase was thrown to the floor, but Alison still sat right where Nicole had put her. The doll looked on at the carnage of our bedroom with unblinking eyes. I looked at the doll and a chill ran up my spine. Something in the doll's expressionless face made me uneasy.

Nicole and I spent the next hour putting our bedroom back together. We put all of her jewelry back on the dresser and I folded the clothes and put them all back where they belonged. I found the small golden locket that had come with the doll and put it back around her neck. In all of the excitement I had forgotten all about Nicole's Surprise. When we finally got everything back in place I lay down on the bed and stretched. Nicole walked up to me with her hands hidden slyly behind her back.

"Ready for your surprise?" She asked pulling a small box out from behind her back where she had been hiding it. I sat up and took the box and unwrapped it. Under the wrapping was a long narrow jewelry box.

"Um', isn't this the same box that came with the bracelet that I bought you for your birthday?" I asked confused.

"Hush, just open it up and look inside." Her smile widened as I lifted the lid. Inside the box was a home pregnancy test and a little card. The writing on the card said three words that made my heart speed up and slow down all at the same time. I jumped to my feet and wrapped my arms around my wife.

"Are you sure?" I asked in disbelief.

"I went to the doctor the day before yesterday. Im only two months along but she says it looks like everything is going well." A tear ran down Nicole's cheek as she spoke. We stood there for a long moment just enjoying the sense of being together until we fell asleep in each other's arms.

That night I heard the crying child again. But this time when I sat up in bed the sound was accompanied by the feeling of being watched. I looked around the room and just like before the room was empty. My eyes were drawn to Nicole's bookcase where Alison was sitting. I knew it was crazy but I could feel the dolls glass eyes staring at me in the darkness. Once again the crying stopped as suddenly as it had started. I expected the feeling of being watched to go away with the crying but the silence intensified it. I spent the rest of the night looking into the darkness. Eventually the sun began to filter into the room. The dim light alleviated some of the foreboding from the air.

The next morning when Nicole I told her about the feeling. She laughed at me for letting the doll freak me out so badly. I tried to tell her it was more than that but she persisted.

"You're just not used to having such a life like doll in the bedroom. You were never afraid of Buttons." She teased me picking up Alison and holding her out to me. I looked at Alison's face and tried to convince myself that Nicole was right. The doll was just porcelain and cloth. There was nothing to be afraid of.

"I guess you're right. Maybe the break in freaked me out more than I had expected." I said after a moment's silence.

"Sce? I told you it was nothing to worry about." Nicole took the doll and put it back on the bookcase. I looked at it again and the whole thing felt silly to me.

Nicole had to work so I spent the rest of the day taking down the Christmas decorations and packing them away. Nicole said she didn't want our New Year's party to just be Christmas part two. When everything was packed away I sat down in my favorite chair and opened up the Poe collection that I had gotten for Christmas.

I had just started reading when I heard a sound coming from the bedroom. I sighed as I got out of my seat and went to check it out. The first thing I noticed when I went into the room is that Buttons the rag doll was no longer on the bookcase where she belonged. I searched the room and found the doll stuffed under the bed. The doll had fallen off of the bookcase and rolled at least four feet across the floor. I couldn't figure out how the doll had rolled so far but it was the only explanation that made any sense to me.

Suddenly I felt like I was being watched again, but this time there was a menacing quality to it. I picked up the rag doll and placed it between the pillows on the bed and went back into the main room to read my book. I must have dozed off because the next few hours were a blur.

When Nicole came home she went straight to the bedroom to change clothes. She imediately noticed her rag doll on the bed and asked me about it.

"It fell off the bookcase earlier so I put it there instead. I figured there might not be enough room for both dolls to stay up there."

Nicole just shrugged her shoulders and said, "It's probably best anyways. Alison is more valuable and I wouldn't want to see her get knocked off and broken."

We spent the rest of the evening making plans for New Year's eve. Nicole wanted to tell our families that she was pregnant, but I convinced her to wait a little longer before we did. I told her that we shouldn't tell everyone until we knew the sex of the baby.

"I already know," She said with a wink.

"I thought you couldn't know for sure until the three month mark?" I asked.

"Yeah but a mother always knows. It's going to be a girl, I can just feel it." She put her hands on her stomach and stroked it lovingly. I smiled and put my own hand over hers.

The next two days went by quickly. I was off work through the new year but that just meant I was drafted into the service of my wife. I spent most of my time cleaning the apartment and putting up decorations for the party. When I had free time I would relax and read as much as I could. Nicole helped me with most of the cleaning, but she still had to work during the day which ment I spent most of the day alone in the house.

At night I would try to sleep, but every night like clockwork the phantom crying would start. I tried to ignore it at first, but over time the crying would grow louder. By the second night I had to sleep with headphones on just to drown out the noise. Through all of this Nicole didn't hear or feel anything out of the ordinary. Whatever was going on it was saving it's tortures for me. Eventually I started to dislike the very sight of Alison. I couldn't put it into words, but the doll just repulsed me. I believed that it was responsible for all of the strange feelings that I was having.

For her part Nicole didn't share my aversion to the doll. If anything as my dislike for the thing grew she fell more in love with it. Every night before bed Nicole would say goodnight to Alison as though the doll would talk back.

Christmas Spirits Rueckert

When I woke up on the third day I was startled to see
Alison sitting at the foot of the bed. I tried to convince myself that
Nicole had moved the doll as a joke, but she wouldn't want to
chance the doll being damaged by a fall from the bed. The only
other options that I could think of were disturbing. On one hand I
could have gotten the doll and moved it in my sleep. But I had
never sleep walked before so that option seemed unlikely to me.

The other option was equally unlikely. I knew that there
was no way a doll could move on its own, but somehow It was
sitting right in front of me. I got out of bed and reached out for the
doll. The air around it was sickeningly cold and when I touched it
my hands stung. I ignored the sensation and lifted the doll into the
air to take a better look at it. The eyes that looked back at me were
not the inanimate eyes of a lifeless doll. They burned with a cold
hatred that turned my stomach to look at. The thing in my hand
frightened and disgusted me all at the same moment.

As I stood there entranced by the doll I noticed a slight
movement in the corner of my eye. I looked to where I thought I
saw the movement but there was nothing there. The doll became

colder in my hands and I had to put it down. When I did the phantom crying began, but this time the sound was coming from behind me.

I spun to look for the source of the crying and that's when I saw her. A little girl huddled in the corner of the room crying. It was the little girl whose photo had been in the locket that Alison wore. Her face was even more sunken than it had in the picture. The only life in her face were the dark eyes that pierced through to my soul.

"Destroy the doll." She said in a weak voice.

"I can't destroy it, my wife loves it."

"Destroy it before it's too late." The girl said more firmly. "If you don't then she will destroy you. And then she will take your unborn child."

Before I could respond the girl evaporated in a puff of smoke. I stood there dumbfounded for a moment before I turned back to the doll. It sat staring at me with its blank hateful eyes. I picked it up again and put it back on the bookcase where it belonged. I quickly got dressed and went to the only place I could think of that would have any answers.

When I opened the door to the antique store the first thing I noticed was the smell. On my first visit the room had smelled musty and somehow decayed. This time I smelled nothing but mothballs and cedar chips. It was shocking how much the store had changed in one week. The room was still filled with a miscellaneous collection of old junk, but there was a lighter feeling in the air.

The old man behind the counter smiled as I approached him. But the smile faded slightly when he recognized who I was.

"What can I do for you young man? How does your wife like the doll?" He asked in a tone of forced politeness.

"She likes it fine, I have a few questions about it though." I copied his tone and put on a big smile.

"I told you every thing I know about Her." He put more emphasis on the last word than was necessary. No doubt my calling the doll an it annoyed him.

"I find that hard to believe. I just want to know about the person who sold the doll to you."

"I got her at an estate sale."

"Who's estate?"

"I don't remember." He lied. His eyes darted around the room nervously as he looked for an excuse to end the conversation.

"I don't believe you." I said leaning as close to him as I could. "You aren't telling me everything and I want to know what is going on."

"Have you been hearing things?" The old man asked angrily. "Did you hear the little girl crying yet? That's how it always starts."

"How what starts?"

"Have you seen the girl yet? She's a pretty little thing isnt she? All eaten away from the inside out. The doll did that to her. I never quite figured out how but she did. And now she has chosen you." I tried to interrupt him and ask what I had been chosen for, but the old man just kept ranting. "I can see the circles under your eyes. Haven't slept much lately have you? Soon she'll affect your appetite. You won't be able to eat, and she'll drain you dry just like the she did to the others. She chooses someone then she eats them up bit by bit until theres nothing left." He stared at me with an insane gleam in his eyes. I was suddenly overcome with rage. My hands flew out and caught the old man by the collars of his shirt

"You listen to me you son of a bitch. I will not let this thing hurt my child. Now, you are going to help me figure out how to stop this thing. Because if I die I swear to God almighty that I will take you with me. Do you understand?" When I let go of his shirt the old man took several steps back. He looked at me with frightened eyes for a moment until he appeared to come to a decision.

"You have a child?" He asked after a moment.

"My wife is pregnant, I just found out a few days ago."

"Then there is no time to lose. Alison will want to get you out of the way so that she can take the child before it is born." The old man walked over to the old desk in the corner of the store and beckoned me to follow him. He opened one of the drawers and pulled out a ledger and flipped a few pages. When he found the information he was looking for he handed me the open book. "I bought Alison from a man named Joseph Stewart. He brought her in with a few of his late daughter's old toys. The little girl died of pneumonia when she was six years old. Mr. Stewart told me that he thought the doll was cursed but I never believed him."

The old man turned the page of the ledger in my hands and pointed at another entry. "I sold Alison just six months after Stewart brought it in. The woman who bought the doll went crazy and killed herself two weeks after the purhcase. The police found the receipt for the doll among her effects and brought Alison back to the store along with a few other things. I put Alison in the window and there she stayed until the day you came in. That is all I can tell you young man." He took the ledger from my hands and put it back in the drawer of the desk.

"What happened to the man who sold you the doll?" I asked the old man when he turned to face me again.

"He died not long after I bought Alison. His obituary said it was a heart attack, but I know that it was all Alison's doing."

"The little girl. When I saw her today she told me to destroy the doll."

"She told me the same thing years ago. I tried to but something wouldn't let me." The old man shuddered as if he were trying to push down the memory that his words evoked. "Whatever that doll is, it's powerful and evil. I wasn't strong enough to destroy it, but maybe you can find a way."

I left the store with more questions than I had answers. The old man was obviously insane, but what he told me about the little girl and the doll somehow made sense. By the time I got home I had decided that I had to destroy the doll. Nicole would be angry with me, but I could deal with that if it meant protecting my unborn child. I stopped in the storage area in the basement and then went back up the stairs to my apartment.

Christmas Spirits Rueckert

When I walked into the apartment the temperature had dropped drastically. It was the kind of cold that cuts straight to the bone. I shivered a little as I made my way into the bedroom. The doll was sitting on the bed staring at me with its glass eyes.

When I reached out to lift the doll I felt the same cold sensation that I had before. This time when I touched the doll I I felt as though my hand would freeze, but I pushed down the pain and lifted the doll and lay it down on top of the bedside table. With my free hand , I raised the hammer I had gone to the storage room over my head and prepared to bring it down.

Just as I was about to strike down with the hammer I heard Nicole call my name from behind me. I turned to see my wife standing in the doorway with a shocked expression on her face.

"What the hell are you doing?" She asked as she entered the room. Her eyes were fixed on the hammer I held in my fist.

"I have to do it Nicole, This thing is evil." Before she could stop me I brought the hammer down on the Doll's face. The hollow porcelain head shattered under the blow. Once the head was gone I ripped the body open and dumped its stuffing into the trash. Finally I picked up Alice's locket from the floor and tossed it out the window.

Nicole looked at me in shock. She started to say something but all I could hear was the sound of a little girl laughing. Suddenly I realized that I had just done something horrible. It wasn't the doll that was evil but the little girl. And I had just released her spirit from its prison.

Made in the USA
Charleston, SC
14 December 2011